RUN
JANE
RUN

Also by Maureen Tan

AKA Jane

MAUREEN TAN

RUN JANE RUN

THE MYSTERIOUS PRESS
Published by Warner Books

 A Time Warner Company

Mysterious Press books are published by Warner Books,
Inc., 1271 Avenue of the Americas, New York, NY 10020.

Visit our Web site at http://warnerbooks.com

A Time Warner Company

The Mysterious Press name and logo are registered trademarks of Warner Books, Inc.

Printed in the United States of America

ISBN 0-89296-659-9

To the eight of us who roamed childhood together—
Maureen, Mike, Pat, Shawn, Therese, Tom, Mary, and Martin.
To Mom, who kept us safe.
To Laura and Susanna, who are far too young to be so clever.
To Peter, who is wonderful.
To my children and grandchildren. Ditto.
And to my readers. Thank you.

RUN
JANE
RUN

SUMMER

1

Summertime in Savannah.

Alex and I strolled along River Street, dressed in shorts and short-sleeved shirts, blending with the crowd of tourists and locals moving lazily along the river walk, enjoying the night life and the evening breeze.

Near Abercorn Street, a woman's voice, deep and sultry, drifted from the open doors of the Bayou Cafe. We paused in our walk, lingered nearby, stood side by side as we looked out over the Savannah River, our elbows on the railing, our bare arms touching. The sad, soft sounds of the blues filled the silence between us with a tale of love gone wrong.

"Who's Brian?" Alex asked.

The question, quietly spoken, shocked me.

How did he know about Brian?

I kept my expression bland, the pattern of my breathing unchanged, and looked at him, wondering if he had tried to catch me off guard. He was a skilled interrogator, capable of such a strategy.

Light from a nearby street lamp betrayed the color staining his lean cheeks, revealed only embarrassment. No cunning. He was my lover, not my adversary.

It had been a long time since I'd had a lover.

Ignoring the ache that accompanied any thought of Brian, I said: "He was someone I knew a long time ago. Why?"

Alex's dark eyes darted away from mine, focused on a slow-moving barge. He rubbed the fine white scar that angled above his right eyebrow.

I'd lived with him for five months, shared his bed for four, knew the gesture well. Something was bothering him. I gave him time to work it through, to pursue his line of questioning. Or not. As I waited, I rested my eyes on his face and was struck again by how attractive he was. A storybook hero. Tall, dark, handsome. Intelligent, caring, funny. Trusting. Naive. A street-wise cop and twelve years my senior, yet sometimes he reminded me of a child.

Alex met my eyes.

"Just a minute ago, you called me Brian. You've done it before."

That horrified me. In Savannah, with Alex, my carelessness might cause distress. Elsewhere, it was potentially deadly. I wasted a moment questioning the wisdom of my schizophrenic existence, then resolved to be more careful and focused on the immediate problem.

If I chose not to tell Alex about Brian, he wouldn't press me. Our relationship was on my terms, here and now, my work and my past irrelevant. Alex had accepted that. Since we'd been together, I'd returned to England twice to participate in two short, unremarkable, and necessary operations. One returned a terrorist to prison. The other uncovered a security breach. Each time, I'd returned to Savannah, but offered no details. And Alex had asked for none.

But now he wondered about Brian. My fault. It was best to satisfy his curiosity. Best to end it. There would be no harm in telling Alex the truth, except that I was unwilling to share this most private part of my past. I chose the next words carefully, gave him a different truth.

"Brian was my colleague. He died."

Died because of me. That truth I kept to myself, too.

Alex put an arm around my shoulders.

"You miss him."

A statement. No more questions. No resentment.

Suddenly, there was something else I wanted Alex to know.

When Brian died, I had been certain I would never love again. I was wrong.

But the impulse felt dangerous, so I said nothing.

AUTUMN

AUTUMN

2

Twenty minutes had passed since I'd received the phone call.

Twenty minutes. Like a sleeper caught in a nightmare, I couldn't move fast enough. No matter that I drove with a terrible disregard for traffic signs and speed limits. It still took me twenty minutes. A lifetime.

The emergency room was crowded with men and women wearing indigo blue uniforms. They stood apart from the hospital staff, murmuring to one another in hushed voices, their hands moving over their utility belts, lightly touching leather holsters, walkie-talkies, and polished nightsticks as if they were charms to ward off violence and death.

Conversation stopped when they saw me.

I paused in the doorway, searching familiar faces for some sense of the news to come. I saw only shock edged with fear.

They saw a slim, hazel-eyed woman with curly honey-brown hair who hadn't taken time to change from cutoff blue jeans and a sloppy T-shirt. But if they saw in my face a mirror of their own emotions, it was because I allowed it. Pretty lady authors, even ones who write hard-boiled detective novels, are supposed to show their feelings.

"How is he?" I asked no one in particular.

Suddenly, no one would meet my eyes. Bodies shifted, clearing a path between me and a large, uniformed black man at the opposite end of the room. He sat in a chair beside closed double doors marked Hospital Personnel Only. His face was buried in his hands.

"Sarge," someone said. "Jane's here."

Detective Sergeant Tommy Grayson raised his head, his hands folding around themselves in a gesture that looked like prayer. Blood, nearly dried, dulled the smooth skin of his arms, stained his hands a rusty brown, smeared raggedly beneath his right eye and across a cheekbone.

Alex's blood.

Before Tommy could stand, I slipped into the chair beside him, wrapped my hands around his big wrists and gave them a gentle shake.

"How is he?"

He shook his head.

"I've called Joey. She should be here soon."

Joey was Alex's younger sister. Tommy would not have called her unless——

An aggressive female voice interrupted my thoughts.

"Sergeant Grayson. We heard that Chief Callaghan's been shot. Tell us what happened."

I looked up. Reporters and camera crews were crowding in through the entrance, jostling with one another for position. A young woman wearing the insignia of a trainee was trying to block their way.

Tommy sighed so quietly that I doubted anyone else heard.

"Let 'em be, Jamison. They're just doing their job."

He stood, confronted the cameras.

The lights on the minicams blazed to life.

"I'll give you a statement, folks. Then I'm going to ask that you move outside."

Tommy straightened his shoulders, delivered the information as if it were a routine report. As if his best friend had not just been shot. He chose his words carefully and delivered them precisely. Even his deep Southern drawl, so much like Alex's, lent no warmth to the statement.

"At approximately eight forty-five this evening, Chief Callaghan was the victim of a drive-by shooting that took place in front of the Calvary Baptist Temple on Water Street. No suspects have been apprehen—"

"Hasn't Callaghan been working with rival gangs in that area?" cut in one of the television reporters. Before Tommy could answer, another reporter asked, "Was the attack random or was Callaghan the target?"

"We have no reason to believe that this incident was gang-related. As to whether the attack on Chief Callaghan was deliberate, it is too early in our investigation to determine that or to speculate as to the cause of the attack."

"How is Alex?"

The question came from the pudgy, balding crime beat reporter from the *Savannah Morning News*. He was a frequent visitor to the squad room. In his voice, I heard sympathy.

"He's in surgery." Tommy looked away from the reporters before adding, "We'll keep you posted."

He turned his back on the cameras.

Jamison ushered the reporters from the room.

Tommy sat back down beside me, leaned forward, rested his elbows on his knees, and stared down at his hands.

"The shooter was parked, waiting." His voice was toneless,

as if he was filling in each line of a police report. "We'd just come out of the church. I heard a car start, then heard shots . . ."

I didn't care about the details. I wanted to shake him, to shout at him, to make him tell me, *now*, about Alex. Instead, I sat quietly.

"I dove for cover, drew my weapon as the suspect vehicle accelerated past us. The car sped around the corner."

I knew what he was doing, had often done it myself. The trick was to ignore the pain, to focus on the details.

"It headed east on Lincoln, toward the highway. A late-model Ford Taurus. Dark blue or black. Four-door. No lights."

Tommy's voice faltered. His Adam's apple moved as his neck tensed. He gulped, struggling to control his emotions, trying—and failing—to remain detached.

He hadn't my training. He didn't need it. For him, Vietnam was decades in the past, and Savannah wasn't a particularly dangerous town. He didn't expect those he loved to die violently.

I did.

Sooner or later, everyone I loved—

I dismissed the thought. Alex was still alive.

Tommy took a deep breath and began speaking again.

"I didn't get a license number. Didn't see how many were inside. Couldn't get a clear shot."

He began rubbing at the dried blood on his left palm with his right thumb.

"Alex hit the ground behind me. So at first I didn't realize . . ."

He noticed what his hands were doing and curled them into tight fists.

"I thought, 'Thank God he wore his vest.' Then I looked closer. The bullet'd gone right through. I called for assistance, then I tried to stop the bleeding. Pressed my hand against the wound. Alex was conscious. He tried to laugh. Told me they lied to us in boot camp. 'See, Tommy,' he said, 'Marines *do* bleed.' "

Tommy lifted his head. His eyes glistened with unshed tears.

"I rode in the ambulance with him. The hospital was five minutes away. Only five minutes, I kept telling him. You lasted a goddamn fucking week in the jungles of 'Nam, and you were hurt worse than this. So you hang on, man. You hang on.

"His heart stopped as we pulled into the driveway. They rushed him inside, and I've been waiting . . ."

He shifted his attention back to his hands, unclenched his fists.

His nails had cut crimson crescent moons into his palms.

3

Just hours past his discharge from Candler Hospital, just a week away from almost dying, and Alex lay on the sofa in the living room. His head and shoulders were propped on pillows. His face was drawn and pale.

Joey Callaghan stood nearby, looking down at the brother who had raised her. Although sixteen years separated them and their coloring was very different, the family resemblance was unmistakable. Straightforward dark eyes. High cheekbones. Narrow noses. Stubborn chins.

Joey wore a lime-colored linen dress and matching high heels. A silk scarf swirled with lime and blue was draped around her shoulders. She was blonde, petite, sophisticated. And furious.

I stood by the closed French doors, looking out on a heat-baked day in late September, silently cursing the timing that had brought me into the room at exactly the wrong moment.

"It's about time you thought of someone besides yourself,

Alexander Patrick Callaghan," she was saying. "There are other people involved here. People who care about you. It's about time you figured out something to do in this life that doesn't keep getting you shot."

She paused, arched an eyebrow at me as if I might have something to add.

I didn't.

She frowned, refocused on Alex.

"Be reasonable," he said. "I've been on the force for more than twenty years. I've only been shot this once."

His weak, scratchy voice added worry to her expression, acid to her tone. She held up two fingers tipped with sculpted shell-pink nails.

"Twice. I was there. In the emergency room. Both times."

"Now you can hardly count ol' man Caruthers. He didn't really shoot me. I was just standing in the wrong place when he threw down that shotgun."

She stamped her foot, clearly annoyed.

"Shot is shot. Not only that, you've been stabbed, beaten up, and run over. Now someone's trying to kill you."

He shook his head.

"There's no way of knowing that for sure. Sure, the shooter *might* have been trying to kill me. Or he might have been after a cop. Any cop. Or maybe the shot was fired into the crowd, and I was just the unlucky one. In any event, there's no need to worry. We'll catch the perp. I promise."

"Let someone else catch him!"

Alex made a placating gesture with his hands, tried to sit up, and flinched as wounded flesh, broken ribs protested. He lay back on the cushions and tried not to groan. He didn't succeed.

At the sound, Joey's face went nearly as pale as his. She

stood, hands clenched at her sides, tears welling in her eyes, body trembling, undoubtedly exhausted by the strain of the past week. But she wasn't finished.

"I'm asking you to resign. To go away for a while. Somewhere *safe*. England, maybe. With Jane."

He didn't even glance my way. I would have been surprised if he had. Our relationship was not the issue.

"I'm sorry, Pumpkin. This is my *job*. I won't run away. Not even for you."

His tone and the set of his jaw abruptly brought to mind another situation, another man. I turned my head, stared blindly at the lush greenery beyond the verandah, recalling a darkened bedroom, remembering that I'd been reading in my favorite chair and that Brian had been watching me from our bed. He was on his stomach, his chin propped on his hands, his face in shadow.

"Jane, let's have a baby."

I'd stared at him, startled by the idea. Yet, I could imagine it. I could imagine a wonderfully mundane life for the three of us, a life where a crisis might be a burned dinner or a bumped head or a lost toy. Then I glanced at the report on my lap. Brian's analysis. His proposal. A complex undercover operation in which he would be a key player. He was deliberately endangering his life. Again.

"What about Rome?" I'd asked.

"I have to go. I owe it to Mac. But then, my love, I'll retire."

I'd believed him. I'd begun making plans for our future.

Foolish.

I opened my eyes, looked at Alex and Joey.

She sat on the edge of the sofa, her face buried in her hands, sobbing. Alex stroked her arm, murmured words intended to comfort, and promised her that everything would be all right.

Words and promises just like Brian's.

A single bullet could turn promises into lies.

I fought the impulse to mourn someone who was still alive. One deep breath, then another, and I dismissed the tears. Suddenly, I found myself wanting nothing more than to hurry to the shooting range behind the house, load a clip into my Walther, and take careful aim at a human-sized target. A faceless silhouette. I would pull the trigger. Again and again and again.

I looked down at my twitching trigger finger, at my empty right hand. I, too, was trembling. I was as exhausted as Joey and probably as irrational.

I told myself to get a grip and went to the kitchen to fix us all some lunch.

Weeks passed.

Tommy and Alex created a list of Alex's enemies. Methodically, the SPD located them, eliminated them as suspects, and narrowed the list.

Alex healed. One by one, he reassigned the cops who protected the house and protected him.

I kept alert, turned down an assignment, and fought boredom.

I worked out with Alex, maintaining my fitness, rebuilding his.

And I wrote.

My novels, penned under the name Max Murdock, were doing well. *Pair o' Jax* and *Jax and Diamonds* were newly released in paperback. *Jax of Hearts* would soon be out in hardcover. *Jax Wild* was being considered for a made-for-TV movie. A new manuscript was due to the publisher in a year and, besides that, I needed the distraction.

Andrew Jax tucked a finger between his neck and the stiff collar of his shirt, gave the fabric a tug, then took another swig on his bottle of PeptoBismol.

Weddings and funerals should be banned, he thought. Damn priests should let everyone live in sin and die in peace.

The organ music, sweetly and softly insipid for the past half hour, swelled into the chords of "The Wedding March."

Jax glanced wildly around, seeking an exit.

Jamie McMurphy, Jax's best man, gripped his arm with fingers strong enough to cling to vertical surfaces and pointed past the chapel's half-dozen pews.

"Your bride."

Millie stood at the end of the aisle, wide-eyed, waxen, not moving. Her eyes met Jax's, and she managed one of her brave little smiles.

Jax forgot his own fear.

"Millie," he said clearly. "I love you."

The music reached crescendo.

She stepped toward him. Drew closer. And closer.

A shot rang out.

A red stain bloomed on the white lace between her breasts.

Slow motion.

Her eyes stretched wide with shock and fear. Her mouth moved wordlessly. Her body collapsed, crumpled forward.

Slow motion.

A shout groaned from his lips. He dove, like a diver through water, arms outstretched, hands grasping—— His finger was still on the trigger of the gun he held. Smoke curled lazily from its muzzle.

Slow motion.

Millicent slipped through his arms, past the gun, hit the floor. Droplets of her blood drifted lazily downward, followed the path of her fall, spattered his shoes.

Jax gasped, woke up sweating.

He reached for the fifth of bourbon beside his bed.

Weeks turned into months.

The days grew cooler and shorter.

Alex officially returned to duty.

The list of suspects crept down to one, who was now in prison on other charges. No confession, but Tommy started to concentrate on other cases. And Joey seemed happier.

I had nightmares.

Every night, I awoke, perspiring and afraid. Every night, I sought Alex's hand, threaded my fingers through his just as I had when he lay in intensive care. Then, I'd found more comfort in the warmth of his hand than in the electronics measuring his every breath and marking his every heartbeat. Now, night after night, I lay beside him in the dark, holding his hand and finding only fear.

Thanksgiving Day.

Tommy and his wife, Ginnie, had invited us for dinner. They lived in a sprawling Victorian on Habersham Street, overlooking Whitfield Square. Before we'd got out of the car, Ginnie was at the front door, waving to us. She was wearing an apron over a red blouse and black trousers, and had a baby parked on one ample hip. Another baby was clinging to her leg. She was a big-boned, dark-skinned woman with round cheeks, a cloud of curly hair, and a warm, practical nature. Tommy made no secret about adoring her and their ten-month-old twins, Zach and Tad.

That night, the babies had dinner first, entertaining Alex and me by spreading mashed sweet potatoes and bits of turkey dinner on themselves, each other, their parents, and anything else within range. Then Tommy put them to bed.

We had a delicious meal of turkey and dressing, candied sweet potatoes, cranberry sauce, and string beans. Afterward, we sat in the living room. I settled onto the camelback sofa beside Alex. Tommy and Ginnie sat opposite in a pair of overstuffed armchairs. Tommy leaned toward Alex.

"Did you catch the FBI bulletin on—"

Ginnie reached over and gave Tommy's ear a quick twist.

"Don't you *dare* talk shop in my house on Thanksgiving Day! Especially when we have company. You either, Alex Callaghan! Or there won't be any dessert for either of you."

Tommy rubbed his ear.

"Yes,'m."

Alex wasn't so easily cowed. He lifted an eyebrow.

"What'd you make?"

"Chess pie."

Something nearing ecstasy touched Alex's face.

"I'll behave. I promise. Though I am obliged to tell you that blackmail is a crime in this jurisdiction."

Ginnie laughed and told him he was impossible.

The three of them talked as old friends are wont to do, revisiting childhood, telling stories about youthful exploits and adult experiences, and chatting about events held in common. I listened, limiting my tales to a dozen years of childhood and a few more of university. Beyond that, I shared nothing. I had nothing to share.

The conversation shifted to Christmas plans.

Ginnie, who knew only that I lived with Alex, came from England, and wrote novels, said: "How about you, Jane? Will you spend the holidays with us or go back home?"

I sidestepped the unintentional land mines.

"I don't know yet. Depends more on schedule than anything else."

"It must be hard to juggle friends and family when they're spread over two continents."

I nodded, hoping she was satisfied, hoping to avoid—

"Your folks must miss you," Tommy said.

Too late.

Memory provided razor-sharp fragments from childhood. A foot clad in a polished leather boot, jamming down on an accelerator pedal. A silver crucifix dangling from a rearview mirror, glinting in the sun. Twisted, clawing branches. Sticky blobs of crimson sliding slowly down the windshield, blotting out a cloudless sky.

A long, dark glimpse down the barrel of a gun.

Then, as it had since the day my parents died, memory ended.

"Do you have any other family?" Ginnie asked.

Innocent assumptions were turning ambivalent responses into lies. Lies that I would have to remember and sustain. It was easier in the long run to tell the truth.

"In fact, I don't have any family. My parents died when I was six."

Alex stirred beside me, reached out and briefly caressed the angle of my jaw with his fingers. Love and sympathy from a man who valued family above all else.

"I'm so sorry," Ginny said. "How—?"

Another fragment sliced its way to the surface.

Try to remember! the men kept saying. They spoke quietly, but I knew they were angry. I must have seen something, they kept saying. Didn't I want to help them catch the bad people?

I shook my head, forcing away memory, discouraging more questions.

"Just like Alex's parents. In a driving accident."

Later that evening, I returned from the bathroom to find Alex standing in the living room, holding a fussing baby. Alex's head was bent, his attention completely on the child. He shifted his weight from foot to foot and sang a lullaby softly and unself-consciously, his usual drawl overlaid with a hint of brogue.

"Sure a little bit of heaven fell from out the sky one day,
And it nestled in the ocean, in a spot so far away.
And when the angels found it, sure it looked so sweet and fair . . ."

I lingered, unseen, in the dark hallway, thinking of home and family, of love and belonging. For a moment, perhaps two, I imagined a future. Then I remembered how quickly it could be taken away.

4

Three-forty A.M.

Two days after Thanksgiving.

I lay in bed, wide awake. Again.

Beside me, Alex snored softly, his naked body snuggled against the curve of my bare back, his breath tickling the nape of my neck. Through the balcony windows opposite our bed, the sky was clear, the stars bright. I watched the sky until the threat of dawn diluted the darkness. Exhausted, I nestled my head into the pillows, still reluctant to close my eyes. I was afraid of the images sleep would bring.

Against my will, my eyelids drooped. I slept.

The ringing phone awakened me before another nightmare did.

Eight A.M. on Alex's day off.

Alex muttered something obscene, untangled an arm from the sheets, and nuzzled my cheek as he reached past me. He snagged the receiver from the nightstand, then propped himself up on an elbow.

"Callaghan here."

He stretched the second word into two syllables. *He-ah.* For months, I'd resisted the instinct to imitate his cadences, mimic his speech. This was not an undercover assignment. Survival didn't depend on my ability to vanish, chameleon-like, into another identity.

I sighed, switched on the bedside lamp. Early-morning phone calls to the chief of police generally signaled disaster.

"Hang on," Alex said. "It's for you."

But instead of handing me the receiver, he held it for a moment against his bare thigh.

"A relative. Cockney accent. Young, perky, and female. She giggled, then asked for Cousin Jane. Y'know, it's a real pity to waste that kind of talent on a sleepy cop."

I grimaced.

"Probably a trainee. Practicing."

He shook his head as he gave me the phone. Then he settled back into the bed.

I put the receiver to my ear.

"Jane Nichols."

I heard a click. The woman with whom Alex had spoken was no longer on the line. The voice was Douglas MacDonald's. Very proper. Very British. Very familiar.

"I could use you here, Janie. Will you come?"

The decision was made in the space of a heartbeat.

"Yes," I said.

I desired Alex. Perhaps even loved him. But I didn't have the innocent optimism that life with him required. I doubted I'd ever had it. For months, I'd pretended. For Alex's sake. And mine. I'd tried to believe in happily ever after. But I knew better.

❖   ❖   ❖

Mac spoke for a few minutes, gave me some preliminary instructions. Then he said: "I'll put Miss Marston on the line to make the arrangements."

A stranger's voice with a strong hint of north London and an efficient, unemotional delivery gave me numbers and departure times of flights from Atlanta to London. Computer keys clicked in the background as we spoke.

"Your reservations are confirmed," she said finally, and told me to pick up the prepaid tickets at the counter.

I thanked her, returned the phone to its cradle, and turned to Alex.

Tiny lines had formed between his eyebrows and wrinkled his forehead.

"Leaving again?"

I nodded.

"This afternoon. My flight's at two forty-five. Out of Atlanta."

He began to speak again, hesitated. Then he looked squarely at me and said what was on his mind.

"Are you coming back?"

Once again, he surprised me with his perceptions. A dangerous man. One best left behind. Forgotten. I considered how to answer him and settled on the truth. Cruel, but there was more cruelty in expressing an ambivalence I didn't feel, in offering hope where I knew there was none.

"No, I don't think so."

Pain crinkled the corners of his eyes.

"That's kind of what I thought."

Resignation in the quietly spoken words.

He turned away, pulled the blankets up over his shoulders.

I wanted to wrap my arms around him, to tell him I was sorry.

Instead, I sat up and swung my legs over the edge of the bed.

A faded indigo shirt lay in a huddle beside my pillow. Embroidered at the top of each sleeve in violet, purple, and white was the shield-shaped insignia of the Savannah P.D. Comfortingly soft, the shirt was one of my favorites. Alex's, too. He liked to reclaim it in the middle of the night. I tried not to think about that as I pulled on the shirt and buttoned it. When I stood, it hung well below my hips.

I left the bedroom, padded down the back stairs to the kitchen, put on a pot of coffee, and felt more alone than I had in a long time.

5

The airport clock read 6:45 A.M.

I stood at the edge of the holiday crowd gathered around the luggage carousel, watching an elderly woman. Her tweedy outfit, in shades of heather and cream, was shapeless and practical. Although she was not particularly small, her posture suggested fragility. She and I had met at Atlanta's Hartsfield International Airport and spoken briefly.

"Grammy Wiggins," she'd said, her voice touched with a Scot's burr. "Everyone calls me Grammy Wiggins."

In Atlanta, she'd talked to anyone within earshot, repeating what she had told me. She'd visited a new grandchild in Bermuda, then spent a few days in Atlanta with an old friend, and wasn't the sunshine just lovely. Now she was going home to England. To Brighton, actually. She carried a photo of a fat-cheeked infant, halted the movement of passengers in rows 10 to 27 onto the plane by showing the photo first to the steward posted by the open cockpit door, then to the stewardess standing at the curtain between first and second class.

We'd shared the flight, but not adjoining seats, to Heathrow. She'd preceded me off the plane and positioned herself beside the luggage carousel, between and slightly in front of two middle-aged men. They were executive types, distinctly American, traveling together. They probably had mothers her age.

Grammy Wiggins was not so unsubtle as to actually ask for their help.

Her lips came together in a tight line, her jaw clenched. She made a valiant effort to retrieve her own bag, reached out with hands gloved in buttery calfskin, grabbed at the handle of a battered, hard-shelled suitcase, and held on to it for two shaky steps. The maneuver ran her into the businessman on her left. She released her suitcase with a little cry that was equal parts frustration and pain. The carousel carried her suitcase out of reach.

On its next trip past, her suitcase was snagged by one of the Americans. The two men retrieved their own luggage, then moved toward customs with the elderly woman installed protectively between them.

Obviously determined to keep up with her companions, she lifted her chin, bravely struggling to match their pace. One of her hands clung to the arm of the man on her left. The other hand clutched a voluminous tapestry bag overflowing with knitting needles, skeins of bulky forest-green yarn, and a half-finished sweater.

With a heartfelt sigh, I readjusted my carry-on bag so that its strap wouldn't bite into my shoulder. Then I pulled my suitcase from the rotating belt.

English customs was a madhouse. Lines of squalling children, exhausted parents, and long-suffering business travelers stretched raggedly from each station. The Americans, compelled to abandon their charge for their own queue, first bullied her to the front of the line reserved for British subjects. She smiled gratefully and went so far as to pat one of the men gently on the cheek.

The customs agent should have been alarmed by such overt grandmotherliness. Instead, he waved her through his checkpoint with little more than a cursory glance at her possessions.

I shook my head and sighed again. There were officials in Atlanta and London who had much to answer for. An elderly woman, traveling on a crudely forged passport, had boarded an international flight carrying the components of a bomb.

X-ray scanning in Atlanta should have caught her. But she understood the system, knew its flaws. More important, she understood human nature and knew that the very old and very young are generally treated with indulgence and condescension.

She had waited until the security area was mobbed, its personnel pressured to move passengers efficiently through the checkpoint. Then, as she'd stepped forward in the long line, she'd deliberately snagged her toe on the suitcase in front of her and sprawled headlong, flinging balls of woolly forest-green yarn from her open tapestry bag.

Passengers and security officers scrambled to rescue her, helped her to her feet, examined her for damage, and watched solicitously as she made her way through the checkpoint. Most of her escaped yarn was retrieved, returned to her bag, and x-rayed.

My job was to stand on the far side of the security gate, thumbing through my ticket folder, waiting to act as a helpful bystander if no one else volunteered. I wasn't needed.

One fuzzy ball had rolled through the walk-through security gate, passing below the level scanned by the metal detector. A security officer wielding a hand-held metal detector paused in his examination of a lean, bowlegged man wearing jeans, pointy-toed boots, and a saucer-sized silver belt buckle. In one smooth movement, the officer bent, scooped up the ball of yarn with his free hand, and affected a posture that suggested the presence of a basketball hoop. As the open tapestry bag cleared the scanner, he made the shot and landed the yarn in the bag. The cowboy said, "Two points."

Grammy Wiggins's tumble had propelled another ball of yarn through the narrow space between the walk-through security gate and the bag scanner. It rolled along the linoleum floor until it bumped up against the foot of a grey-haired Atlanta cop. He sat at a small table near a frozen-yogurt stand, cardboard coffee cup in hand, watching the people passing through the security area. He abandoned his coffee, picked up the yarn, walked over to the elderly woman, and leaned in close. After a moment of conversation, he tucked the yarn into her bag, showed her to the chair he'd just vacated, and spoke into his walkie-talkie. Within a few minutes, Grammy Wiggins was settled into a wheelchair and whisked to the departure gate.

She boarded the airplane and, throughout the flight, added row after row of stitches onto the tubular body of the bulky sweater she was knitting. Beneath the first row of yarn was a thick needle made from a length of flexible linear charge. At the core of one of the balls that had rolled through security was a timing device. The lethal combination—minus a key step—was assembled within minutes in the privacy of the washroom, taken back to the cabin, and set.

The elderly woman disembarked in London, but left the bomb beneath her seat. The aircraft and many of its passengers continued on to Copenhagen. If she had been a terrorist, the flight would not have reached its final destination.

*   *   *

As Grammy Wiggins cleared customs and hobbled out of sight, I joined the only short line in the complex. Though a half dozen pilots and stewardesses were ahead of me, the line moved rapidly. Within minutes, I handed my passport and foreign-office-issued identification to a young man. He had the muscles of a bodybuilder, close-cropped ash blond hair, and a smile that conveyed more enthusiasm than his job required. He looked as if he might be old enough to shave.

I was thirty-four.

"Welcome home, Miss Nichols."

The invitation to flirt was more in his eyes than his words.

Did he flirt with every woman who passed through his station? I wondered.

I offered him my most endearing smile.

The dimples in his cheeks deepened. He lifted his cleft chin in the direction of my closed suitcase.

"Did you enjoy your trip? Anything to declare?"

"Nothing. And I'm delighted to be back. London weather is so pleasant this time of year."

Londoners were being treated to their fourth week of overcast skies and drizzle. But as he waved me through the checkpoint, he chuckled at what must have been a very tired joke.

The elderly woman smiled as my luggage and I joined her in the backseat of a cab. With a minimum of cursing, the cabby, who had a bulldog's jowls and a gold front tooth, wedged the cab into the heavy stream of traffic moving toward central London. Then he switched on the radio. Willie Nelson was singing a twangy country-western rendition of "Rudolph, the Red-Nosed Reindeer." Within moments, his voice was joined by the cabby's Cockney-accented baritone.

Grammy Wiggins held out a gloved hand.

"Pay up, Janie."

The words were spoken quietly, for even a world-weary London cabby would be curious about a male voice issuing from an old woman's face.

"Bah, humbug," I murmured to my fellow operative and sometime partner, John Wiggins.

His acting ability had cost me twenty pounds.

I counted out the notes.

6

The cab from the airport let me out at the southwest end of Lambeth Bridge. We'd already dropped John at his flat. Lucky sod. All the way from Heathrow, he'd talked in his little-old-lady voice about a hot shower and a long nap. I'd finally told him to belt up.

I avoided the Thames House's main entrance on Millbank. There, on the bustling first floor, the organization maintained its public face. Conservatively dressed men and women labored in offices clearly labeled as to purpose. Nameplates were common on desks, counters, and lapels. Prompt and courteous service—"Her Majesty's subjects are our best customers"—was the goal.

I went in through a side entrance instead.

Even then, it was impossible to walk into the Thames House without sensing a larger, perhaps even noble, purpose to the activity there.

Twenty-four hours a day, seven days a week, three hundred sixty-five days a year, MI-5's staff of nearly two thousand full-time employees devoted themselves to the tough job of ensuring national security. All within an annual budget of two hundred million pounds. I'd once heard a young woman from the public relations office say that as she shepherded visitors through the cavernous stone building. She'd spoken in the rapt voice of a true believer, then gone on to describe MI-5's five specialized branches.

Her explanation somehow brought to mind a hive of Africanized bees. Some protected the hive from within, watching for breaches, working to keep the internal structure strong. Others were part of an outwardly directed swarm, potentially lethal, but focused on nonviolent activities.

A handful of us made the most agitated swarm seem benign.

That handful worked for Mac.

I passed a familiar checkpoint and went upstairs, avoiding the elevator for fitness' sake. I arrived on the fifth floor only slightly out of breath, and walked unrecognized but unaccosted through a maze of hallways and offices. On the upper floors, anonymity was the norm, paranoia a reflex. The labyrinth corridors were populated by strangers moving purposefully between doors that were unlabeled and often unnumbered.

Some things had changed over the years. Remodeling had brought modern business sensibilities to the upper floors—improved lighting, new carpeting, computers, and ergonomic work areas. About bloody time, I thought, remembering hours spent sitting on a wooden chair under a bare bulb typing reports on a machine older than I was.

Recently, the remodeling had extended into the area that Mac directed. The tiny, familiar offices had been painted eggshell white and carpeted in beige. The desks were new but, as usual, few were occupied. This morning, I saw only one familiar face. I lifted my hand in greeting, then walked into Mac's two-office suite.

I knew that Mac's secretary, Arlene, had retired, but the reality startled me. From my first days with the organization, she'd been there, white-haired, plump, and much given to polyester with ruffles at the neck. She had guarded Mac's door, dispensing common sense, pieces of caramel, and occasional scoldings as the situation demanded.

Now a stranger was in her place. The woman who sat at the desk was close to my age, taller and thinner, had café au lait skin, a heart-shaped face, and glossy hair pulled back tight. She wore a jade green silk blouse and a sleek woolen jumper.

I smiled, introduced myself.

The smile that was returned didn't reach her eyes. Didn't travel beyond the slight upward curve of her lips.

"We've spoken," she said. "I'm Miss Marston."

Then she asked about my health and the flight in a tone clearly intended to evoke no response. As she pushed the intercom to announce my arrival, I glanced around the office, looking beyond the new computer, matching file cabinets, and streamlined desk. I was struck by what was missing. No plants. No family photographs. No knickknacks. The work area suited Miss Marston—expensive, impersonal, and efficient.

I wondered if Mac missed Arlene, too.

Miss Marston showed me into the interior office and closed the door behind me.

I found it comforting that modernization hadn't reached this far.

Weak incandescent overhead lights were supplemented by brass table lamps. The burgundy and brown Turkish carpet betrayed the room's traffic patterns. The leather on the arms and seats of the dark green office chairs had been rubbed to a dull yellow-brown. And the office still smelled pleasantly of pipe tobacco, leather, and wood polish.

Mac sat behind his desk.

I smiled warmly, spontaneously, pleased to see him.

Old habits die hard.

I was the last of a generation of operatives indoctrinated from childhood, then cultivated through adolescence. The last of a generation who regarded immediate superiors as something more than employers, something more than associates. Mac had recruited me thirteen years earlier over dinner at his club. He'd spoken of duty, honor, and loyalty. Of obligation and family. He'd told me my grandfather would have been proud.

The newest generation learned of MI-5 through the pages of glossy booklets filled with photos of plush offices, squash courts, and young, attractive staff members. They read about career opportunities, salary, and employment benefits. They were promised fun, excitement, and challenge.

The organization offered whatever it thought recruits would buy.

Reality, for all of us, came later.

"Hello, Mac," I said quietly.

He looked up from his papers, over the tops of his bifocals.

"Good morning, Jane."

His smile was brief, perfunctory. It was followed by a long, hard look across an expanse of polished mahogany. Not hostile. Assessing.

Quite reasonable.

I'd been gone for several months. It was his job to evaluate my fitness. I'd conducted similar assessments of operatives I planned on sending into the field. It was essential to know how much pressure they could bear before they broke.

I stood quiet and relaxed under his scrutiny and amused my-self by looking back. I noticed the lines around his mouth, the shadows beneath his eyes, the tension in his jaw. His skin was pale and wrinkled, delicate rather than weathered. And the color of his close-cropped grey hair was less steel, more winter than I remembered. He was old, I thought suddenly. Well be-yond the age of mandatory retirement.

Apparently satisfied with whatever *he* saw, Mac stood and walked around the desk.

"Come in, my dear. Sit down."

I heard warmth and approval in his voice, saw it in his smile.

There was a time when that had been compensation enough for my periodic forays into hell. Now I understood the manip-ulation behind it and entered hell only on my own terms.

He waved me toward the chair in front of him, then turned away for a moment to push some papers back from the edge of his desk. The movement presented me with a profile—high forehead, aggressive nose, determined jaw. A hard man. My eyes sought the portrait that hung above his desk. It showed a woman at the height of her power. Elegant. Regal. Proud. No softness in that profile, either. I wondered whether Mac's length of tenure was by his choice or Her command.

Mac cleared his throat, interrupted my thoughts. He leaned back against his desk, folded his arms across his chest, looked at me.

"Tell me about the flight."

My brief report was received by a minute's worth of steady, quiet, non-repetitive cursing. Ex-Royal Navy and a former field operative, Mac's vocabulary was formidable. Finally, he sighed.

"Unfortunately, it's about what I expected. A half dozen teams came back with reports like yours. And ground trans-portation is, as always, much worse. Officially, security around airports and train stations is tight. In fact, it's abysmal. Short-staffed. Neglected. Sloppy."

He handed me a sheaf of papers and waited as I thumbed through them, looking at points-of-origin and destinations and the security disasters in between.

I shook my head as I handed the papers back.

"It'll be a miracle if we make it through Christmas without incident."

"I want the problem fixed, Jane. Now. Make contact with the appropriate organizations. Don't bother with the bureaucrats at the top. Go to people like yourself, people who will act first, deal with the paperwork later. Tell them who's out there right now, waiting to take advantage of their security lapses. If anyone asks, your instructions come from the PM himself."

He shifted, turned a shoulder toward me as he set the reports back in the center of his desk. Then he took his pen from the holder and jotted a note on a yellow pad. He spoke as he wrote.

"By the way, how much time can you commit to us this trip?"

"As much as you need. I'm moving back into my London flat. Permanently."

Mac held his pen poised.

"You won't be returning to Savannah?"

"No."

Extraordinary how difficult it was to keep emotion from coloring that one, short word.

Mac finished the note with a familiar flourish of initials, then looked back toward me.

"I'm sorry," he said.

And he managed to sound as if he meant it.

WINTER

7

Two days before Christmas found me in Mac's office again, in one of the leather office chairs in front of his desk, listening intently, increasingly appalled.

"John will act as your second," Mac said finally.

I had no objection to the partner, just the assignment.

At the request of a senior Member of Parliament, Mac wanted us to rescue a young man from armed kidnappers. Sir William Winthrup's nephew and only heir, Hugh, was being held on the family estate in northern Scotland.

During Christmas week, the manor's only occupants were a housekeeper, Eupheme Beane, and her seventy-year-old father, who served as groundskeeper and handyman. Usually. But a fortnight earlier, nineteen-year-old Hugh had argued with his uncle, left London in a fury, and gone to the house in Scotland. Within days, Miss Beane delivered a ransom note to Sir William's London offices. A nondescript white envelope had enclosed the square of white paper. The message was short, handwritten in black ink.

£5,000,000.

*   *   *

I looked away from the ransom note at the center of Mac's desk, met his eyes, and spoke without heat.

"It's a distressing situation to be sure, and my sympathy is with Sir William. But the police have people specifically trained for this. They won't appreciate MI-5 interference."

Mac shook his head sharply.

"The police will not be involved. William came to me—to us—because he suspects that his nephew is cooperating with his captors, that he may, in fact, have engineered the scheme himself. William doesn't want his only heir to end up in prison."

I knew Mac too well to be taken in. He wouldn't involve the organization in anyone's domestic problems. Even unofficially.

I frowned.

He gave it another try, spoke in a voice laced with patience—a teacher answering a bothersome question posed by a precocious student.

"If this organization is to survive, Janie, it *needs* powerful allies. Like William. Money is tight, and the threat of Soviet subversion has ended. Some MPs are challenging the need for a Security Service. With each budget hearing, the threat grows. William supported the Security Services Bill and backed us against Special Branch when we requested greater authority in the fight against Irish terrorism. We gained a larger share of the budget as a result. Now, with the Yard claiming we mishandled the Docklands bombings incident—"

"We *did* mishandle it," I said mildly.

Mac's shoulders stiffened reflexively. He lifted his chin.

"There were circumstances—" Then he caught himself. "We need William's support, now more than ever. At this point, a scandal would be disastrous for him. And for us."

I moved on to more practical matters.

"How fond is he of the nephew?"

"Not very. But it would be impossible, of course, to avoid an investigation and adverse publicity if something were to happen to the boy. So Hugh will need protecting. Miss Marston has arranged transportation to Scotland for you and John. You'll be met there by a special security unit. Eight men."

I reached into my purse for a pack of cigarettes, tapped one out, lit it, and took a long drag.

Predictably, Mac frowned.

Inconvenient for him if I died of lung cancer.

"Why so many, Mac?"

I made the question sound more casual than it was.

He wasn't fooled. He didn't answer.

I butted my unsmoked cigarette in the nearby ashtray, stood.

"Give me a call when you're tired of playing games."

Mac leaned across his desk and favored me with a blue-eyed stare.

"Sit down, Jane. Please."

I perched on the edge of the chair, waited.

"We can't always choose our allies," he said. "I've agreed to help William. For the sake of the organization. I've told you everything he told me."

"You don't trust him," I said flatly.

Even in the privacy of his own office, he wouldn't admit it.

"I'm concerned the situation may become . . . complex. It could require extra resources. That's why I'm sending you."

8

The eight young men carried HK MP5 submachine guns. Somehow, the dark van in which we traveled suited them.

We had met them on Christmas Eve at an airfield in northeast Scotland, near the Grampian Highlands.

Actually, we only met their leader.

He'd waited until the small plane that had carried John and me from London took off again, then crossed the tarmac to where we stood beside our gear.

"I'm Hawkins," he said.

He was a burly man, in his mid to late twenties, with the curly reddish-blond hair and the broad, open face of a Welsh farm boy. His fatigues had no insignia, but his right hand twitched as he suppressed the urge to salute.

John noticed that, too. He waited until we were out of earshot, carrying our cases of delicate electronic equipment to the van, then murmured: "Who dares, wins."

I nodded, recognizing the SAS motto, agreeing with John's assessment, wondering who owed Mac a favor.

"I'll lay odds he's carrying a new five-seven in that underarm holster," John continued. "I suppose it would be cheeky to ask to see it."

FN Herstal's 5-7, touted as one of the most powerful handguns in the world, was capable of penetrating forty-eight layers of laminated Kevlar armor at a range of two hundred meters. The handgun was lightweight, with virtually no recoil. An effective weapon when confronting terrorists wearing body armor.

An effective weapon when confronting a *cop* wearing body armor.

The thought came out of nowhere, brought with it a chill that had nothing to do with the outside temperature. The 5-7, so new to government organizations in the UK, was already sold illegally on the streets of the United States. Too easy to imagine the face of a particular police officer who could be threatened by that gun.

I dismissed the memory of Alex lying still and waxen in intensive care, then looked at John and produced a credible grin.

His weapon of choice was a Browning 9mm. Nearly eight inches long and weighing two pounds, it had a twenty-round magazine and kicked like a mule.

"Pistol envy, John? Surprising, considering the size of yours."

John snickered.

We loaded into the van and drove into the night.

A storm was blowing in.

Difficult to know whether to curse or applaud. Heavy clouds gathering over the moon's bright face would give us darkness. Predicted snow would turn the footing dangerously slick.

Ignoring the bite of the wind, I peered through the darkness in the direction of the Georgian manor house, considering the grounds and the tall stone walls, and hoping that the north side of the building would offer options that did not exist on the east, south, or west.

The house was oriented eastward, with a grand entry at the center and massive stone chimneys on either end. In front and in back, first- and second-story walls were broken by generous windows outlined in pale granite. The clear panes were framed by stained glass cut in a distinctive diamond pattern. On the north and south walls, stockade-style windows—deep-set and narrow—flanked the chimney stacks. On the third floor, east-facing dormers broke the steep pitch of the slate roof, and stingy windows brought sunlight into servants' quarters, abandoned for decades.

I lifted night vision binoculars to my eyes and explored a half dozen possible routes across the grounds. It was easy enough to dismiss all possibilities save one. John and I could make it, I thought. If we were careful. And lucky. I retraced the route, memorizing its details.

The wind gusted again, reinforced by icy droplets. Bare branches rattled overhead. Dead leaves swirled around my booted ankles and scuttled out across the lawn.

A light went out behind a window on the north wall, returning my attention to the manor house. At almost every window on the second floor, a sliver of light showed above the drapes. Throughout the night, the light behind one window, then another, would be extinguished briefly as someone with binoculars looked out over the grounds. The rotating sentries made it impossible to know how many there were or to predict which window might be chosen next. One thing *was* certain. These were no amateurs who had invaded Sir William's house.

The light came on again.

I stepped away from a laser transmitter that rested on a tripod near my elbow and negotiated the two meters of brushy undergrowth separating me from John.

He stood among the sparse branches of a young pine, his dark clothing making it difficult to pick him out of the shadows. We were dressed much alike. Our silk turtlenecks were warm without being bulky. Leather jackets and loose trousers of tight-woven fabric offered some defense against knife blades and thorny branches. Soft leather boots with thick rubber soles provided traction and support without limiting movement. Neither of us wore a bulletproof vest. They were too cumbersome.

Padded headphones covered John's ears. His shoulder supported the butt end of a tripod-mounted laser receiver.

I touched his arm.

He slid his eyes toward me, lifted an index finger, and raised an eyebrow.

I nodded, complying with his mute request. I could wait.

He refocused on the house.

For the past two hours, we'd worked our way along the edge of the manicured lawns and formal gardens, pointing the laser transmitter at line-of-sight windows, illuminating the glass with a beam of light undetectable by the human eye. Sounds behind the windows vibrated the pool of invisible light, creating interference patterns in the reflected beam. The laser receiver read those patterns and converted them back into sounds.

Our fingers and toes might be near-frozen, but thanks to technology, we had a better fix on the problem confronting us inside Winthrup Manor. We still hadn't located Hugh, but from listening in on snatches of conversation, John and I had estimated that there were no more than ten people in the house, most of them congregated on the first floor. The only innocent victim of the kidnapping was in the kitchen at the back of the house. I was determined to keep Archibald Beane alive.

The last time the housekeeper had seen him was just before she'd left for London to deliver the ransom note. He was at the kitchen table, his hands bound in front of him, a noose tucked under his flowing beard. The end of the hanging rope was thrown over an exposed ceiling beam, anchored to one leg of the table. One of the kidnappers had spent a moment demonstrating how easily the rope could be pulled taut.

John pushed the headphones down around his neck and turned his head toward me.

"Got the little sod! Master Hugh is in his bedroom. And if he's a prisoner, I'm the Queen Mother. But he's definitely unpopular with the fellow at the window."

He paused, stepped away from the equipment, flexed his shoulders, then continued.

"Loud music on the second floor masked Hugh's half of the conversation, but I doubt it could be anyone else. I heard, 'What are you doing in the hallway?' A pause, then the same voice again. 'Very well. I'll have Dickie bring you a tray.' A longer silence. Then, 'His royal frigging highness is hungry.' Pause. 'Only way he'll keep his bleedin' arse in that bedroom.' So someone on the second floor has a walkie-talkie. Or there's a house phone."

"Nice work."

"Thanks. So now that we know Hugh's upstairs and the old man's in the kitchen, I suppose it's time to solve the problem of getting across the garden."

I passed him the binoculars, pointed.

"I've been thinking about just that. Take a look. Hedgerow, flower bed, fountain, spruces, foundation."

No need to mention the wide stretches of lawn in between.

He aimed the binoculars, adjusting brightness and focal length with fingers gloved in supple black leather. Beneath the gloves, his scarred and mutilated hands were a reminder of how badly things could go wrong.

John spent a moment tracing the route, grunted noncommittally, lowered the binoculars, and glanced at the sky. The moon broke through the clouds. Its light touched his face, turning his fine blond hair silver, draining the color from his pale blue eyes, and transforming his narrow features into an expressionless mask.

For a moment, he looked like the killer he was. Passionless, distant, efficient. Just as he'd been trained. He might occasionally be my partner, might often work for Mac. But, ultimately, John answered to someone higher in the organization. Someone whose name I didn't want to know.

The wind gusted. Darkness consumed the moon and the illusion.

John handed back the binoculars.

"What then, Janie?"

What then? indeed, I thought.

I tried to sound confident.

"I'll climb the north wall, cross the roof, go in through a window, creep down to the second floor, take out the sentry, and secure young Hugh. You sneak around to the back of the house, get as near as possible to the kitchen. Maybe even slip inside. Once in position, we each signal Hawkins. Then I protect Hugh and you protect Miss Beane's father from the bad guys while our people storm the front gate. Simple."

The sound that John buried in his collar was somewhere between a disbelieving snort and choked laughter.

The wind moved from gust to steady gale, lowering the temperature several degrees. I shivered, gave the zip on my jacket an upward tug, hoping for additional warmth, but finding that the zip was already at the top.

John took the headphones from his neck, hung them over the end of the receiver. The wind was strong enough to set the headphones swinging. He stretched again, linking his fingers behind his back, arching his back, pulling his shoulders toward his spine.

"This weather makes my bones ache."

"Old age, Grammy Wiggins?"

Fifty-two, wiry-tough, and deadly, John was far from old, fragile, or sweet.

"I'm too old for *this*."

The sweep of his hand took in the overcast sky and the manor house. I couldn't be sure if he was referring to the weather, the operation, or both. I decided it was best not to ask.

"Let's walk away from this one, Janie. Something's not right here. Leave it to the hooligans from Hereford."

When I didn't answer, he sighed.

"Well then, I suppose your way is as good as any."

I looked at the sky, checked my watch.

"We'll go in thirty minutes. I'll brief Hawkins. You coming?"

"In a bit. Leave the binocs, would you?"

By the time I reached the rendezvous area, it was sleeting.

John and I had tucked the rest of our gear beneath a lightning-struck elm. I hunkered down beside the charred trunk, dug through my pack for a waterproof poncho. Before I'd finished shrugging my way into it, Hawkins had detached himself from the darkness.

"Breaching the house won't be easy," I said. "The only reasonable approach is across the formal garden to the north wall. With luck, their sentry won't look out a north window at the wrong moment."

"We can neutralize that threat. A sniper—"

I shook my head.

"No. We can't risk confrontation until we're inside the house. If we're spotted crossing the grounds, John and I will not return fire. Neither will you."

"You and your partner could end up bleeding on the lawn—"

"Then you'll pull back, report, and await instructions."

"Leaving you both to die?"

"If need be."

"I don't like it."

Despite our whispers, I heard the scowl in Hawkins's voice. Not surprising.

Men like Hawkins were good soldiers. Training might move them into an elite section of the Royal Armed Forces, make them extraordinarily effective, but it didn't change their basic nature. They remained good soldiers, loyal to their unit, unlikely to walk away from fallen comrades.

My training had not been as kind.

I raised my chin, narrowed my eyes, delivered each word with precision.

"If we fall, you will pull back, report, and await instructions. Understood?"

He didn't snap to attention, salute, and bark, "Yes, ma'am!" But his whisper managed to imply that response.

* * *

I was leaning forward, re-strapping my throwing knife over my right calf, when John arrived.

Hawkins gasped at his sudden appearance.

I stifled a chuckle, then carefully pressed the last Velcro strap into place. After testing the sheath's fit, I gave my pant leg a tug and straightened.

"There's an old coal chute at the back of the house," John said without preamble. "The boards covering it are rotted. According to Miss Beane, there's a door up from the cellar directly into the kitchen. She said she'd installed a 'wee latch' to keep the cat from prying open the door and creating a draught."

I nodded, remembering how patiently John had listened as she'd described the elderly calico cat and its peculiar behaviors in minute detail, as if this information, too, could prove vital to the rescue of her father and Hugh. And I supposed it had.

"I'll wait in the cellar, close to that door, and set my shoulder to it when the time is right."

"Good," I said. I looked at Hawkins. "Once we've signaled, you and your men can cross the garden, storm the house. After that—"

"Yes, ma'am. We know what to do after that."

No hesitation in his voice. No enthusiasm, either. Just absolute surety. Hawkins and his men were good soldiers. They would do their duty for God, Queen, and country.

Hawkins moved off to gather his unit.

I stepped in front of John, curled my right hand into the supple leather of his jacket, gave it a quick shake.

"You crossed the garden. Twice. With no backup. Don't you ever learn?"

In a rare display of affection, John raised his gloved fingers to my cheek.

"You care too much, Janie. A bad habit."

Minutes earlier, I had insisted that Hawkins leave John to die.

Duty made monsters of us all.

9

The rain was falling in an icy torrent.

We huddled against the damp foundation in a corner formed by the north wall and the chimney.

John was not happy.

"Insanity. You can't climb in this."

No point in letting him know I wasn't particularly keen on the climb either.

"We have merely achieved what the Scots call 'full conditions.' Invigorating. Nothing more."

I stripped off my poncho and jacket, exchanging dryness and warmth for mobility, and reminded myself that exertion would cure my goose bumps. Then I traded my boots for smooth-soled rock-climbing shoes and pulled on a pair of fingerless gloves.

John spoke again when I took a pair of wool socks from my kit and tugged them on over my shoes.

"What's that in aid of?"

"Better footing. It's an old Joe Brown trick." Joe Brown was an English hardman of legendary rock-climbing ability.

I rechecked the closure on my belt pouch, the strapping on my two-way radio and throwing knife, and the soft webbing harness that held my Walther PPK Special and its Brausch silencer under my left arm.

Then I turned my attention to the wall. I set my left foot on one of the wall's rough-hewn blocks, reached above my head and curled the fingers of my right hand into a mortar line between chimney stones. And climbed.

John waited below, ready to protect my back or to scrape up pieces. As the situation required.

The world narrowed to fingers and toes, to minuscule cracks, bumps, and edges. Awareness of the distance between me and the ground melted away, replaced by awareness of my body and its relationship to the section of wall within reach of my hands and feet. I moved steadily, kept three points of my body in contact with the wall at all times, using my free hand or foot to stretch, grab, step, or push.

I reached the overhanging roof and edged my way along a line of mortar until I was clinging only to the chimney. Ignoring the steady flow of icy water down my arm, using the angle between the chimney and the roof line as an anchor point, I pulled myself upward until I could see the slate shingles that angled steeply to the roof's peak. Then I took a breath, reached along the side of the chimney, groped for finger holds. Found one. And gained the rooftop.

I stood with my back to the chimney, muscles quivering, senses heightened, momentarily unaffected by the wind howling around me, tugging at my wet clothing, driving icy rain into my uplifted face. I wanted to shout into the darkness, to announce to the elements that I, Jane Nichols, had defied gravity and death. Again.

It occurred to me that, under the circumstances, the announcement might be a trifle premature. So I focused adrenaline-inspired energy on crossing the slick slate roof. Compared with the vertical ascent, slab climbing was easy. I placed all my weight onto the balls of my feet, letting the wool socks and friction work for me. I moved quickly and confidently toward the dark shadows of the first dormer.

Too quickly. Too confidently.

I slipped. My feet went out from under me, and I landed on my side, began a steady slide down the 40-degree slope. I rolled onto my stomach, used hands and feet as brakes, exposed as much body and clothing as possible to the slate surface. I slowed to a stop. My feet were within inches of the roof's edge.

I *hated* climbing.

I half-crawled the several feet remaining to the dormer, maneuvered my way around to the window, stepped onto the sill. It was hinged on the left, latched on the right. I dug in the pouch, pulled out the proper tools. In less than a minute, I cut the glass, undid the latch, and swung the window open. It swept the sill, forced me to spend another unpleasant moment balancing on the angled slate rooftop. And then I was inside.

I stood motionless, listening, and heard nothing suspicious. Using a penlight's narrow beam, I examined the room. No closets. No furniture. Just cobwebs, dust, and a bare bulb hanging from cloth-covered wire. I walked through the open door into a narrow passageway that dead-ended immediately to my right in a cramped bathroom. With my back to the bathroom and peering into each room along the way, I walked the length of the corridor to a small landing. A steep flight of stairs took me down to a closed door.

I tucked my torch away, retrieved the Walther from its holster. After threading my finger through the trigger guard, I pushed the door open and found myself alone in the second-floor hallway near the end of the south wing.

I closed the attic door behind me. Except for an unobtrusive brass knob, it was indistinguishable from the polished mahogany panels lining the wide hallway. The panels glowed, warm and ruddy under the subdued light of crystal wall sconces.

I walked toward the center of the house.

Thick carpeting in shades of cream, maroon, and cobalt blue covered the floor. Massive bedroom doors, solidly shut, broke the walls at regular intervals. Between the doors were long, narrow tables—carved affairs with marble tops. Heavy chairs upholstered in silk damask stood beside the tables.

Elegant. Except that the hallway had been vandalized. The cream-and-shell-pink striped fabric covering the chairs was slashed. Horsehair stuffing was everywhere. A dark wad of it, like the corpse of some small animal, was caught on the jagged teeth of a broken liquor bottle that lay in the middle of the hallway.

On the walls, life-sized oil paintings of the Winthrup ancestors had not escaped attack. I glanced at the nearest portrait. A long-dead Winthrup glared back, oblivious to the ragged slashes that marred his finery. There was something odd about his eyes, but I didn't look more closely. Instead, I smiled ruefully as I passed, thinking that if he were able, he would cover his largish ears with his hands to protect them from the slashing, discordant music blaring from the north wing.

An open foyer at the top of the formal staircase separated the two bedroom wings. I crept across it, sparing a glance over

the railing at the brightly lit reception hall below, then continued on.

The destruction in the south wing was repeated in the
north. Graceful ebony stands had once filled the spaces between doorways, supporting a collection of vases. The stands
were splintered, the vases smashed. Ignoring the impulse to hug
the wall, I walked down the center of the hallway, stepping over
furniture and glass, holding the Walther down by my thigh. I
counted doorways. Hugh's was the fifth on my left, nearly to
the end of the corridor. Hopefully, a sentry seeing a figure
moving at a normal pace would hesitate for a moment before
attacking. That moment would be enough.

It very nearly wasn't.

I was almost to Hugh's room when a dark-haired man
emerged from the doorway opposite. His glance traveled past
me, snapped back in a classic double take. His Uzi swung in my
direction.

I crouched, pulled the Walther's stiff trigger, felt the semiautomatic buck in my hand, heard the muffled sigh of the silenced shot. The fellow's neck and head erupted, spattering the
wall and ceiling behind him. He crumpled to the carpeting,
oozing a dark stain onto a field of cobalt blue flowers.

The Special had a seven-bullet clip. One bullet used. Six remaining. The mental tally was automatic.

I dragged the body into a nearby room, then went back to
Hugh's bedroom. I twisted the knob, found the door unlocked,
and dove into the room, tucking my body into a roll that carried me off to the right and gave me a split second to survey
the scene. I found my footing and stood. My Walther was
clenched in both hands and aimed squarely at Hugh's chest.

He was oblivious to my presence.

The heir to the Winthrup fortune sat cross-legged and

naked in the center of a massive four-poster bed like some huge, pale bullfrog. Close-set eyes, closed for the moment, were set in a large, pimply face. Straight brown hair hung down on his forehead and covered his ears. Music blasted from six-foot-tall speakers located in the corners of the room and on either side of his bed.

If it had been quieter, I could have heard him sniffing. As it was, I had only the evidence of my eyes to know that he'd just snorted a line of coke. A small mirror with a smudge of tell-tale white powder and a thin straw lay on the nightstand. Beside the mirror was the open, fist-sized bag.

I was horrified to find myself shouting over the music.

"Hugh!"

No response.

I held my Walther out of sight, stepped nearer the bed, touched his bare shoulder with my left hand. His eyes opened. They were pale brown, the irises liberally flecked with yellow.

I stared, startled by the unusual color and the certainty that I'd seen those eyes before. Hugh stared back, open-mouthed, his surprise mirroring my own. Then his mouth and chin tightened into the familiar lines of the Winthrup family portraits. I remembered that some of those eyes were the same peculiar color.

"Your uncle sent me," I shouted.

"Sod my uncle. Stingy wanker. I wrecked his precious treasures. Now we're really going to make him pay."

Then the Winthrup features softened into a leer.

Hugh's tongue touched his upper lip as his eyes did a slow trip over my body, my wet silk turtleneck undoubtedly exposing more than it hid. An erection grew between Hugh's flabby thighs.

"They promised to take good care of me, but you're quite a surprise."

He shifted forward, grabbed at one of my breasts.

I slapped his hand away, leveled the semiautomatic at him.

His smile froze, faded. Passion withered.

"Get dressed."

He slipped from the bed as I glanced around the room. Heavy furniture. A closet. An open door to the bathroom. No lock on the bedroom door. Even so, I could easily defend our position. Assuming it needed defending. As long as we stayed put, and the music continued blaring . . .

The man hiding in the bathroom made the mistake of moving during a two-beat rest.

I'd been careless.

He was slow.

I dropped to the floor, fired twice. My bullets pierced the door, then his body. His scream blended with the music. Then he was silent.

Four bullets remained.

Hugh sprinted past me, still naked. He ran from the bedroom, yelling for help.

I scrambled to my feet, raced after him.

He was young and had a head start, and we both had to avoid the glass littering the floor. But I was fit. I caught up with him as he reached the foyer, before his shouts could be heard over the music. Mötley Crüe, I thought inanely as I tackled him, ramming my shoulder into the back of his knees and toppling him forward. He kept crawling, difficult to stop but now blessedly silent. His panic took him across the foyer. I followed, finally grabbing him by the hair. I wound my fingers in it and forced him to his feet.

When I let him go, he stood, red-faced and gasping, tears streaming down his cheeks.

I didn't want to risk crossing the foyer again, and Hugh's bedroom was now farther than the attic. I'd take him there, put another set of stairs between us and trouble. I held the Walther at waist level, pointed it at Hugh, lifted my chin to indicate direction. No resistance. He marched forward to the sounds of a screaming chorus: *Knock 'em, knock 'em, knock 'em dead, knock 'em dead, kid . . .*

I glanced behind me, pulled the radio from my belt left-handed, pressed the transmit button.

"Primary target secure—"

A man came into the foyer, his Uzi held point up, obviously not expecting trouble. He saw us. And died. His finger spasmed on the trigger, bullets unaimed, ineffective, loud. No way the music could cover the sound.

Three bullets left.

I swung back on Hugh.

The abrupt movement saved my life.

He held the broken liquor bottle, undoubtedly intending to plunge its jutting edge into my neck. As it was, I saw the murderous look in his yellow eyes as his blow drove the bottle's razor-sharp edge through the flesh and muscle of my right upper arm, slashing it to the bone.

Reflex took over in the critical moments before my brain acknowledged the injury. I slammed the radio transmitter across his exposed wrist. As he dropped the broken bottle, I tried to secure the transmitter to my belt. When it slipped from my fingers, I abandoned the task. I transferred the Walther to my left hand and aimed it point-blank at Hugh's crotch.

"Attic. Now!"

I followed Hugh down the hall the remaining few meters, opened one of the bedroom doors as we passed by, and smeared the knob with blood, hoping the ploy would buy an extra minute or two.

Hugh located the inconspicuous brass knob, yanked the attic door open, and took the steps two at a time. I closed the door behind us and followed him.

With the point of the gun, I urged Hugh past the empty rooms, into the bathroom at the far end of the passageway. There was barely enough space inside for the two of us. To our right, an old loo. Behind the door, a pedestal basin. Directly before us, a claw-footed cast-iron tub. Blue enamel on the outside, grubby on the inside.

I prodded the fat roll at Hugh's waist.

"Into the tub. Face down."

His large body was tense with outrage. But he sniffed deeply, straightened his back, and climbed in. He folded his legs beneath him as he pillowed his face against his arms.

The music cut off abruptly.

I left the bathroom door open, wedged myself into the cramped space between bathtub and toilet. Cursing whoever had removed the lid and seat from the toilet bowl, I braced my left arm along its cold porcelain edge and sighted down the passageway to the small landing.

Now that I wasn't moving, pain no longer ripped through my arm. It throbbed in angry rhythm with my heart. I looked at the red mess dripping from my fingertips onto the dusty white-tiled floor. Undoubtedly, the bastard had nicked an artery. I had to stop the bleeding.

First, I had to reload.

I glanced over my shoulder. Hugh hadn't moved. Yet.

I ejected the nearly spent clip from the Walther, muffling

the sound with my body, then pinned the semiautomatic against the floor with my foot. I retrieved a full clip from my belt pouch, loaded the Walther, picked it up again.

Seven shots.

How long, I wondered, before they realized we were in the attic, before they picked out the telltale droplets of blood from the pattern on the carpet?

Behind me, Hugh stirred.

I waited, gauging his progress by the sounds he made, and fired as he lifted his head. The bullet whizzed past him, buried itself in the wall, sprayed him with plaster and splinters of wood.

One bullet gone. Six remaining.

I aimed point-blank at Hugh's face. And for one dizzy, crazy moment imagined that *I* was looking into the barrel of the gun.

If I didn't remain lucid, I'd be too dead to worry about blood loss.

I tightened my grip on the Walther.

"There *is* an alternative to rescuing you."

Color drained from his cheeks. His eyes widened. His mouth formed a slack O.

I knew exactly how he felt. Maximum vulnerability. The certain knowledge that death would come screaming from the depths of that long, dark cylinder.

I waited, let terror build, then offered a reprieve.

"Down. Now."

He obeyed.

I thumped the tub with the butt of my gun.

He whimpered, huddled in deeper.

It would take a few minutes before desperation made him stupid. That would be time enough.

I laid the Walther on top of the cistern, fumbled the belt from around my waist, fed the leather end through its buckle, slipped the resulting loop up over my arm, above the biceps. I pulled the belt tight, wound its remaining length around my arm again, and threaded it through itself to secure the tourniquet.

I retrieved my weapon.

I didn't faint.

Someone at the base of the steps shouted.

I peered down the passageway with eyes well adjusted to the darkness.

The rush of footsteps on the stairs paused before reaching the landing. They moved cautiously after that.

I waited, heard movement, glimpsed a shadow and pulled the trigger twice. My first shot missed. The second found its target.

A man tumbled into the passageway.

Four bullets.

Two men followed the dead man through the doorway and used his crumpled body for shelter. A volley of bullets ricocheted off the bathroom fixtures. Behind me, Hugh screamed as a bullet was deflected by the tub.

Muzzle flashes gave me something to aim at. I fired. The fellow on the left fell. His mate huddled behind the improved cover of two bodies.

Three bullets.

The sharp, abrupt explosions of flash-bang grenades signaled that the assault team had arrived. Had the kidnappers remained downstairs in the main area of the house, the grenades would have stunned them. Unfortunately, I'd drawn most of them to the second floor, south wing. They were trapped unless Hugh could be recaptured and used as a hostage.

The fellow attacking my position grew desperate. He sprayed the hallway with machine-gun fire, then dove for the doorway into one of the abandoned rooms. He landed dead.

Two bullets.

Downstairs, the distinctive sound of government-issue MP5 submachine guns combined with the clatter of Uzis.

I shifted to relieve the cramping in my legs. Managed to bump my right arm against the edge of the loo. I bit down hard to keep from screaming. The dim passageway blurred, wavered, and came back into focus with sick-making abruptness. I wiped my face against my left shoulder, braced my cheek against my extended left arm.

Hugh flung himself onto my back.

He clamped his fingers around my throat, tried to force my head into the few inches of water at the bottom of the bowl.

"Up here! I'm up here!" he shouted.

I dropped my Walther, grabbed blindly for his back, caught a handful of hair. I wrenched him forward with all my might, bucked my body upward, flung him over my shoulders. He slammed flat against the tile floor, air whooshing from his lungs, and lay very still, head near the loo, legs sprawling through the bathroom door.

I retrieved my Walther, staggered to my feet, stepped over him, and flattened my body on the hallway floor, leveling my semiautomatic.

Just in time.

Another attacker came into view. I fired. He crumpled.

The fellow behind him stopped short, dropped his weapon, and raised his hands.

"Don't shoot. Please."

I'd never killed an unarmed man. Or woman.

And I had only one bullet left.

It took me a moment to make my mouth form the words I wanted.

"On the floor! Face down! Hands behind your head!"

As I followed his rapid downward movement, the walls on either side of him undulated toward the wavering rectangle at the end of the passageway. I tried to refocus. Couldn't.

I heard a groan, wasn't sure if it was mine or Hugh's.

Another shadow moved.

I shot at it.

No more ammo.

I doubted I'd have the opportunity to load another clip.

"Miss Nichols! Hold your fire!"

The urgent voice belonged to Hawkins.

I lowered my weapon.

The bare bulb in the passageway came on, flooded the scene with 40 watts. Two men rushed into the passageway, intent upon my captive. They bound his hands behind him, checked him for weapons, pulled him into a sitting position. I'd created a problem by leaving him alive, I thought. I doubted any of the other kidnappers had survived.

It didn't matter. As long as I followed *my* orders. If Hugh talked to anyone, he could let loose the very scandal his uncle and Mac were trying to avoid. So no one besides John or me would be allowed near him until he was taken away by private ambulance to a remote sanatorium.

I dragged myself into a sitting position, braced my back against one wall, and slid my feet forward, effectively blocking my end of the hall.

The walls and floor tilted threateningly.

Resisting the temptation to close my eyes, I rested my left

elbow on one bent knee and let my wrist relax so that the
Walther hung, point down, between my legs.

Hawkıns pushed past his men, moved toward me and
Hugh.

"Everything's under control. Let me see to—"

He came too close. I lifted my Walther, aimed it.

"Back away."

He took two quick steps backward, hands raised, palms
outward. Turned his head, shouted over his shoulder.

"Maccoby! Clear our people from this hallway. And get her
partner up here. Now!"

Awareness washed out. And in. And out. An eccentric tide as-
saulting a black sand beach. The cough of a silenced weapon
broke the rhythm, pulled me back. Then I heard John's voice.

"Dispose of this. With the others."

A rush of footsteps responded to his order.

Problem solved, I thought. The last kidnapper was dead.
No prisoners, no charges, no testimony, no scandal. Duty
done, debt paid.

Beside me, Hugh was groaning his way to consciousness.

Ugly prick. Let John cope with him.

"Janie."

I made the effort, opened my eyes.

John knelt beside me, pale blue eyes intent on my face. His
hand was outstretched. I stared at it, uncomprehending.

"Give me the gun, Janie."

I'd forgotten I had it, didn't have the strength to lift it.

"Take it. No bullets anyway. Bad guys got 'em all."

I thought it was rather a good joke. Tried to laugh.
Couldn't.

John didn't laugh either. He took the Walther from me, laid it on the floor, away from the blood.

I couldn't understand why he looked so grim.

My arm didn't hurt anymore.

Nothing hurt anymore.

I closed my eyes. Ignored the conversations around me, the touch of a stranger's hands tending my wounded arm.

Nagging thoughts.

"John?"

"Yes, love."

His voice seemed to have moved. No matter.

"Is Mr. Beane all right?"

John laughed.

"Oh, yes. He's a tough old blighter and as big as a house. I came through the cellar door, thinking I was going to rescue him. But he'd already gotten his arms—wrists still bound— around his guard's neck. He snapped it like a twig, then grinned at me and muttered, '*Ceud mile fàilte.*'"

It was a traditional Celtic greeting. "One hundred thousand welcomes."

I smiled, attempted to drift away.

But an odd idea formed at the edge of awareness, demanded attention, snapped my eyes open. I needed to tell John before I forgot.

The medic was kneeling where John had been. John was on his feet, leaning against the wall opposite me, posture casual. Except that his Browning was pointed at a spot a few feet to my left.

"Hugh," I said.

John shifted his eyes to my face, fractionally lifted the Browning's muzzle.

"Still here. The ambulance is on its way. In the meantime, I'm hoping he'll give me an excuse—"

Hugh moaned.

I didn't turn my head, didn't look at him. Didn't *want* to look at him.

"He was there," I said. "In Greece. He killed my parents."

Spoken aloud, the accusation made no sense at all.

I was thinking just that when consciousness abandoned me.

10

Music from a radio at the nurses' station drifted through the open door to my room. Christmas Day evening, and a choir was singing about good King Wenceslaus. The volume was low; memory provided most of the lyrics.

I swung the Formica tray-table aside, moving the remains of Christmas dinner out of reach, and settled back against the cranked-up head of the hospital bed. I eased my body into the pillows. From my left arm sprang an IV line, anchored to the top of my hand by a wide piece of sticking plaster and ending in a bag of electrolytes hanging from a portable stand.

My right arm was wrapped, shoulder to elbow, in a thick layer of bandages and supported by a sling. I wasted a moment sourly contemplating the wrapping job, wishing I were ambidextrous. Shooting left-handed was a survival skill I had struggled to acquire. Otherwise, I was chronically, pathetically right-handed. If the wound didn't heal properly . . .

I took a deep breath, rotated my shoulder and wiggled my

fingers, ignoring the pain, seeking reassurance. Everything moved as it should. Thanks largely to Dr. Bowers.

She had stitched up my arm early in the morning, told me how lucky I was to have reached the clinic within six hours. Longer than that and—assuming I hadn't bled to death—infection would have made stitching inadvisable. As it was, a little intravenous rehydration, antibiotics, and some skilled needlework—absorbable sutures in the deep part of the wound; a neat, closely spaced series of nylon sutures on the surface—had done the job.

But later that morning, Dr. Bowers had frowned as she'd visited me in my room.

"Don't underestimate the damage that's been done. That arm will take time to mend. If you're careful, the stitches can come out in a fortnight. Then the muscles will have to be rebuilt. Plan on a month or two of physical therapy. After that, well, we'll see."

She'd wished me a Happy Christmas and gone home to her family.

Unfortunately, the nurse's aide was still on duty. Exhaustingly maternal and chronically cheerful, she was much given to unnecessary plumping of pillows and smoothing of blankets. After refilling my pitcher with ice water, she shifted her attention to my dinner plate, measuring the leftovers with a practiced eye.

"Were the brussels sprouts too difficult for you to manage, dear?"

The brussels sprouts had been overcooked, mashed almost to oblivion, and studded with clots of margarine. A backward toddler could have managed them, but the poor little bugger would have been put off vegetables for life. I resisted saying so, simply shook my head.

The aide clucked sadly, clearly taking the rejection of the brussels sprouts personally. A silent moment or two passed as she figured out that I wasn't going to eat them to make her happy. She tugged ineffectually at the upper edge of my blanket, finally cleared the tray-table.

"You'll feel better after you've rested, dear. Is there anything you'd like before I go off shift? No? Shall I close the door?"

The room was a small one, with barred windows and a single door. Silly, but I didn't want my escape route blocked.

"No. Just leave it." I dredged up a smile. "And Happy Christmas."

Past the meager distraction of supper, a tedious evening stretched before me. I considered how I might use the time productively, decided to nap. I pulled the chain that switched off the light above my bed, groped along the edge of the mattress until I found the buttons that dictated its angle, and lowered the head of the bed. I rolled onto my left side, rearranging the pillows to support my injured arm, and closed my eyes.

My arm ached. No combination of bed, body, and bedding offered relief. My mind darted restlessly from thought to thought, remaining long enough to create anxiety, never long enough to offer resolution.

I thought of Alex. Thought about calling him. I could wish him a Happy Christmas. Good excuse to hear his voice again. I could tell him—

Exactly what?

That I hurt, and I wanted him to hold me? That nothing had changed since I'd seen him last except I'd killed a few more people, and how was the weather in Savannah?

I shifted my right arm until the sling was taut and the bandages tugged at the edge of the wound. The pain was effective distraction.

My attention shifted to Winthrup Manor. I thought about what we'd encountered there, about the men who were now dead. Wondered what Hugh had gotten himself involved with. Unlikely that the men we'd killed were cronies of Hugh's. Or merely thugs. They were too well armed, too well organized. Too professional. It was almost too bad that John had killed the last of them. Mac might have pried some interesting information from him.

That thought took me to the moments before I lost consciousness. Delirious, I thought. I had been pain-wracked and delirious when I'd claimed that Hugh murdered my parents. They'd died long before he was born. Undoubtedly, Mac would hear of my accusation during the debriefing sessions. He would dismiss it just as I had.

Still, the idea lingered, nagged at the edges of my mind.

It followed me as I slipped into the clutches of sleep.

Andrew Jax was driving the limousine, and the road was rough.

I sat beside him, jouncing on the leather seat, and my dream-mind knew I wasn't really me. I was dressed strangely—a scoop-necked white blouse, a tight red skirt, nylons, and high heels.

The interior of the limo was hot. Not surprising. Flames consumed the backseat and in the midst of them—

I looked away, out at the road, at the canopy of moss-hung trees.

"Lock the door, Millie!" Jax shouted. "Lock the door!"

As I reached for the lock, the door flew open.

At the same time, hands from the backseat grabbed the back of my blouse, tried to pull me to them, drag me into the flames.

I screamed, threw myself through the open door, out onto the steep rooftop. I flattened myself against the wet slate shingles, but I slid downward anyway. My feet went over the edge.

I flung out my hands, caught the corner of the chimney. Dug my fingers into the line of mortar between the bricks. Stopped moving.

I looked upward.

A man stood at the peak of the roof, staring at me, his yellow eyes set in a face of swirling darkness. He pointed. Down. Past my feet.

"Remember, damn you! Remember!"

I turned my head. Saw below me a shattered window. Its ragged teeth glittered with blood.

The chimney crumbled beneath my hands. Disappeared.

I began sliding again.

Legs, hips, torso, out over the edge. I scrabbled at the wet slate with my fingers, left bloody trails as my nails tore away.

I slid. Screamed. Fell down and down and down and down.

Falling.

I jolted awake, gasping, heart pounding.

A dream. It was only a dream.

I groped for the light, switched it on.

I breathed. I forced emotion away. I watched the second hand sweep the face of the clock a half dozen times. I examined the room's floral wallpaper and identified ten species of flowers in the printed bouquets. Eventually, I was calm. But lingering fear and too much adrenaline made sleep impossible.

I searched for distraction at the nurses' station just beyond my room. There, a miniature Christmas tree and a few brightly wrapped packages vied for counter space with file baskets and a couple of telephones.

Behind the counter, a burly male nurse with dark beetle brows and chronic five o'clock shadow sat with his back to me. His name was Sid, and his attention was absorbed by a bank of twelve television monitors decorated with red velveteen bows and loops of evergreen garland. Only two of the tiny black-and-white screens glowed on. They showed the interiors of the wing's two occupied rooms.

Earlier, I'd wondered aloud about the other patient. The nurse's aide—eager, perhaps, to convince me that I was quite well off—shook her head, clucked her tongue, told me the patient down the hall was in a coma. So tragic, she said. Such a young man. With a lifetime ahead of him. She couldn't imagine what he'd been thinking when he swallowed those pills.

I could.

It was not a train of thought I cared to pursue.

I slid from the bed and, wheeling my IV stand with me, wandered the small room and looked out the barred windows, killing time.

The magazine rack behind the bathroom door finally provided the distraction I needed. As I sat on the stool, I sifted through the contents of the rack. I took a stapled report back to bed with me. *Patterns of Global Terrorism* was issued annually by the U.S. State Department and generally made for boring reading. But scrawled on the pages of *this* copy were scathing comments, pointed corrections, and rude cartoons. Handwriting varied and ink colors changed throughout, but the editorial perspective of the added comments was distinctly British—or at least distinctly MI-5.

I had gotten as far as the section on state-sponsored terrorism, was smirking over a colleague's comment on American paranoia over Cuba—"You Yanks might try living next door to Ireland"—when there was a tap at the door.

I lifted my head, put the report aside.

Mac stood in the doorway, the knuckles of his left hand still on the doorjamb, his right hand fisted at his side. He wore a navy blue sweater and dark trousers. His eyes were on me, his expression unreadable.

He crossed to my bedside.

"Happy Christmas, Janie."

He opened his right hand, held it palm upward, offered me a tiny box wrapped in silver paper and tied with a fine gold cord. Every Christmas for as long as I'd known him, he'd given me a package much like it.

We'd known each other for a lot of Christmases.

Mac had been a frequent and welcome visitor to my grandfather's home. When I was eight, Mac taught me to play chess. At ten, he stopped letting me win. On my fourteenth birthday, he gave me a BRNO .22 caliber semiautomatic rifle, then coached and cajoled me until my accuracy rivaled his. When I was almost nineteen, he stood with his hand on my shoulder and tears on his cheeks. Together, we watched as my grandfather's coffin was lowered into its grave.

I took the silver package from Mac's outstretched hand.

For a moment, I held the small box enclosed in mine.

For a moment, I wished for things I didn't have.

Then I gave the gift back.

"Thank you. But I can't—"

Trust you. That's what I intended to say. I can't trust you. But it was Christmas, and I was tired and I hurt and I wanted to believe, at least for this day, that Mac's manipulation of me hadn't begun in my childhood, that he really *had* cared about me.

"I can't—unwrap it myself," I said.

Just a few steps from my bedside was a maple occasional table topped by a stubby porcelain lamp and flanked by two over-stuffed chairs. After switching the lamp on, Mac extinguished the overhead light, then settled into one of the chairs. A tiny silver fox, forever poised and alert, stood on the polished table-top beneath the lamp. The light, which etched dark lines on Mac's face, glinted brightly off the fox.

I lay against the pillows, relaxed and quietly admiring work-manship that could breathe life into metal. The fox was a lovely addition to the menagerie of silver animals Mac had given me over the years. I kept them in a carved rosewood box, tucked into a bureau drawer in my London flat.

"It's beautiful. Thank you."

"You're welcome, Jane."

Mac pulled his pipe and tobacco pouch from a pocket, then dug around in the drawer of the table until he found an ash-tray. In defiance of the signs posted all about the clinic, he lit his pipe.

I watched him, enjoying the familiar ritual.

For years, Mac kept a supply of his favorite tobacco on a shelf in my grandfather's study. Each Christmas, my grandfa-ther would take me into the tobacco shop in the village where I would buy enough Black Aromatic Cavendish to fill Mac's humidor to the brim.

I still gave him tobacco for Christmas. It had become a token gift, ordered by phone months in advance, paid for with plastic, wrapped by a stranger, delivered by messenger. Efficient. Impersonal. Cold.

A sudden ache in my chest brought tears to my eyes. I turned my head away from the lamplight, not wanting Mac to see them. They were nothing more than convalescent tears, I told myself. Quick to flow. Meaningless.

I cast my mind back through childhood, searched for a memory that would reawaken humor. I found it, found the energy to grin as I faced Mac again.

"Do you remember the Christmas when I *made* you tobacco?"

"Oh, yes." Mac smiled, crossed his long legs at the ankles, took a long drag on his pipe, exhaled. "An intriguing blend of chopped purple medic, ground apple, and molasses."

I laughed.

"I worked hard to achieve the proper color and texture. Bobber approved the flavor." Bobber was my fat Welsh pony. "And it *did* pack well into your humidor."

That memory led to others, and we talked for a time about Christmases long past, recalling the people and animals populating my grandfather's country estate. When the discussion turned to cats, I said:

"Kitty-mou was always my favorite."

"A more self-satisfied cat I've never met. Wasn't she a Christmas kitten?"

I nodded.

"From Grandfather. My first Christmas in England."

My first Christmas without my parents.

11

Mac was telling me about a Christmas decades in the past.

"I looked into my Christmas stocking, fully expecting, and bloody well deserving, nothing more than lumps of coal. It was filled with gob stoppers. Certain that a mistake had been made and the candy would soon be whisked away, I stuffed as many pieces as I could into my mouth. Just then—"

I was grinning at the image of a young Mac with bulging cheeks when Sid interrupted us. A holstered semiautomatic hung from his belt, a gaudy Father Christmas tie was vivid against his white uniform. He checked my temperature and blood pressure, announced that the first was too high and the second too low, and made notes on my chart. He left the room briefly, then returned with two pink tablets in a tiny paper cup and a hypodermic filled with a clear yellowish liquid.

I wrinkled my nose.

"More antibiotics?"

He nodded, poured me some water, handed me the tablets,

watched me swallow them, then emptied the contents of the hypodermic into my IV.

Mac followed him into the hallway. As Mac lingered by the door, Sid walked out of my line of sight. Minutes later, he returned, accompanied by a stranger.

Mac showed the man into my room and pulled the door shut behind them. They approached my bedside, the stranger remaining a half step behind Mac.

Mac began introductions.

The stranger stepped forward, leaned over my bed, and smiled.

Yellow eyes stared down at me, trapping me against the pillows.

My stomach twisted in a painful, icy spasm. I gasped, raised my bandaged arm defensively, pressed my body into the mattress, clawed at the bedclothes with my left hand.

Sir William Winthrup hastily stepped away from the bed.

"I'm so sorry, Miss Nichols. I didn't mean to startle you."

Unrestrained emotions revealed too much, betrayed weaknesses, vulnerabilities. I couldn't afford them. I lowered my arm, unclenching my fingers from the bedding, forced myself to look straightforwardly into Sir William's face.

He was sixtyish, of average height, substantial rather than overweight. Thoughtfully styled reddish-blond hair shot through with ash camouflaged large ears and minimized the length of his face. A ginger-colored mustache separated thin lips from an aquiline nose. And his eyes were like Hugh's. Pale brown, liberally flecked with gold. Not feral yellow.

That was irrational. Childish and irrational.

Didn't matter. I stared at him wide-eyed. Terrified. Unsettled enough that the sound of Mac's voice startled me.

"She recognizes you, William. From Greece."

Sir William's florid face went pale.

"After all these years?"

Mac nodded.

"She made the connection when she saw Hugh. First time she's shown any hint of remembering that whole affair. She thinks you killed her parents. I believe that it's essential to clarify the situation, don't you?"

Mac didn't wait for Sir William's reply.

He retrieved the fox from the table and held it out toward me. It stood on tiny silver feet in the palm of his hand.

"The fox is pretty, isn't it, Janie? Bright and pretty."

I couldn't help myself. I nodded.

Mac brought his hand closer, held the fox inches away from my face, let his hand drift slowly right, then left, then right.

"Watch it carefully. You don't want it to get lost."

Part of my mind was shouting, demanding attention. I ignored it, followed the fox with my eyes.

"Relax, Janie. You're safe here. Safe and secure. Relax."

I continued staring at the fox.

"Who are you afraid of, Janie?"

Against my will, I looked away from the fox. My gaze traveled to Sir William. Yellow eyes stared back at me from a blank mask of a face.

Something was wrong. I was losing control.

I found a coherent thought, willed myself to hold on to it, managed to gasp it out.

"You drugged me?"

Mac didn't answer. My question slipped away into the fog that had become my mind.

"You've seen those yellow eyes before, Janie. You were just a wee lass, sitting in a tall chair, your legs dangling well above the floor. You were wearing a sundress. White, with tiny navy blue dots. And the room, Janie. A table at its center, a mirror along one wall. I want you to remember that room, Janie."

Suddenly, I couldn't breathe. My pulse raced, my heart pounded.

"Mama! Papa! Make him go away!"

The cry, shrill with terror, came from my lips. But the voice was that of a child. I tried to slide off the big chair—

No! Madness! I was in a bed, in the organization's clinic. I tried to struggle up from the pillows.

Mac reached out, brushed damp tendrils of hair away from my face. His gentle touch and the comfort of his familiar voice soothed away panic.

"You're safe. Don't be afraid. Just relax. I'll protect you. Go back to that time, Janie. Go back . . ."

I was a big girl.

Mr. Bennet told me that. Six years old was big enough to answer important questions properly. Big enough not to cry.

I wasn't crying.

I sat quietly, sandaled feet dangling above the floor, hands folded in my lap. He sat across from me, asking the same questions the other men had asked. Between us was a heavy metal table with two neatly tucked-in chairs on either side.

Mr. Bennet's tall, shiny forehead was wet. The bright, bare bulb above the table made the drops glisten.

"You saw an old, black car."

"A Mercedes."

Whenever Mama was very busy, Stavros and I would wait at a sidewalk café, sipping lemonade, naming the different kinds of cars that passed by. I was good at the game.

"A Mercedes pushed you off the road?"

"Yes. We crashed."

Mr. Bennet put his hands, palms down, on the edge of the table and leaned forward. He raised an eyebrow.

"And then?"

I pressed my lips into a tight line, spread my fingers wide, looked at my fingertips.

"What happened then, Jane?"

His voice was quiet. He was pretending to be nice. But I knew he was angry. Because it was my fault. If I had locked the car door—

I laced my fingers together, knuckles out, fingers between my palms. Right pinkie, left pinkie. Right ring finger, left ring finger. Right bigman, left bigman. Right pointer, left pointer. Just like in a nursery rhyme Papa had taught me.

"I asked you a question. Please answer it."

I lifted my hands so that they were in front of my nose, stared at my thumbs. Coral pink thumb nails, side by side, pointed upward. I'd painted my fingernails with Mama's favorite nail polish. She'd laughed when I showed her that we matched.

"Jane!"

I kept my hands in front of my face, touched my index fingers together so that they pointed upward, too.

"Here is the church. Here is the steeple."

I spread my thumbs wide.

"Open the doors."

I flipped my hands outward, away from my body, palms upward, fingers stiff.

"Shoot all the people."

Mama and Papa and Stavros. If I thought about them too hard, I would cry. If I thought about them too hard, I would remember.

I didn't want to remember.

Mr. Bennet's chair scraped loudly as he pushed himself away from the table. He stood, stalked to the other side of the room, stopped in front of the big, wide mirror. He looked at his reflection, then shook his head, frowned, turned his back on the mirror. He dug in his pocket, took out a pack of cigarettes. Lit one.

"The man in the mask pointed his gun at you, too, didn't he?"

"Yes."

Mr. Bennet took a long drag, blew a stream of smoke toward the toes of his brown wing-tip shoes. Mama said cigarettes were bad. Stavros smoked when she wasn't looking.

"What did he say?"

"We leave this life at the whim of Atropos."

Mr. Bennet's chin jerked upward as his eyes focused on me. He took a step, hesitated. His voice was excited.

"The man in the mask said Atropos ordered the hit?"

"No. Stavros said it. I told him cigarettes could make him die. He laughed and told me about the Parcae." I said the word carefully, as Stavros had taught me.

Mr. Bennet still looked confused.

"The Fates," I said patiently. "Clotho holds the wool. Lachesis spins the thread of life. Atropos cuts it."

Mr. Bennet's face cleared. His shoulders drooped.

"Very good, Jane. Now tell me what the *man in the mask* said when he pointed the gun at you."

I pursed my lips, pitched my voice low. The English accent was familiar, easy to imitate.

"Sorry, love. You weren't supposed to be here."

"Why didn't he shoot you?"

Mr. Bennet said the words slowly, softly.

My head hurt and my stomach ached, but I thought about it hard.

"I don't know."

Mr. Bennet blew on the tip of his cigarette until it glowed red. Then he put it back between his lips and looked at me again.

"When the car caught fire, there must have been smoke. Thick, dark smoke. Did it smell bad? Did you cough very hard?"

I shook my head.

"I don't remember."

"Did you see the car explode, Jane? Or were you already running away? Perhaps you heard only the noise? Did it hurt your ears?"

"I don't remember."

A tear tickled my cheek. I wiped it away with the back of my hand. Another tear. I wiped it away, too. I was too big to cry.

Mr. Bennet took another drag on his cigarette, sighed deeply as he exhaled. When he spoke, he seemed to be talking to himself. He sounded tired. Very, very tired.

"The child is traumatized, Mac. Give her time. Perhaps then—"

"Intolerable!"

The shout came from the other side of the mirror.

I heard noisy footsteps, and the door to the interrogation room was flung open. A man with reddish-blond hair and a pencil-thin mustache burst in, rushed toward the table. A few steps behind him was another man, tall, with very short hair.

The man with the mustache grabbed the front of my dress, pulled me from the chair, lifted me until my face was level with his.

I stared into his eyes. They were yellow. Bright. Angry.

"You were there. Their blood was all over you!"

He kept shaking me.

"Your mama. Your papa. Dead. And you. Here. Alive. You must have seen something."

The tall man was shouting.

"William! Put the child down! Put her down, I say!"

Sir William brought my face close to his.

"Remember, damn you."

His hissing voice was almost a whisper.

He let me go.

I scrambled under the table, hid between the legs of the tucked-in chairs.

"Sod that bloody temper of yours, William. You've terrified her."

The tall man knelt down near the end of the table, ducked his head to peer in at me.

"Hello, Janie. My name is Mac. I knew your mama and papa. And I know your grandpa, too. He's an old friend."

His voice was nice. His face was wrinkled but not really old. His eyes were bright blue. He held out his hand, smiled a thin, crooked smile.

"Come out of there, lass. I'll keep you safe."

A rustling noise made me look over my shoulder.

Sir William was on his hands and knees, reaching for me. He grabbed my ankle.

"Got the little bugger!"

"No! Mama! Papa! Make him go away!"

I kicked his hand.

He caught my other foot, dragged me from beneath the table.

I couldn't get away.

I covered my face with my arms, screwed my eyes shut.

Inside my head, I screamed the words that kept me safe.

"I don't remember. I don't remember. I don't remember."

Around me, the room was silent.

The drug left my system, sapping my remaining strength as effectively as it had sapped my will. Memory remained vivid. For a time, I lay against my pillows, barely moving, blindly staring at the ceiling.

Not for long.

Moving from anguish to anger was easy, really. Similar transformations took place daily, often creating front-page news. Love turned to hate. Guilt to aggression. Sorrow to rage. I had been trained to consciously manipulate those feelings. In myself and others.

Anger brought insight.

I turned my head, looked at Mac. He was back in one of the bedside chairs, smoking his pipe, reading a week-old edition of the *London Times* by lamplight. We were alone. After apologizing for his boorish behavior of three decades earlier, Sir William had left for London.

"Why?" I said.

The word was barely audible and greeted with silence.

I repeated the question, volume unimproved.

Mac looked up from his paper, spoke around the stem of his pipe.

"Later. Sleep first. You're exhausted."

"Now."

How could so much fury carry so little volume?

"Very well."

Mac moved his pipe to the ashtray on the table, rested his arms along the overstuffed arms of the chair. Brown age spots stained the pale skin on the backs of his wrists and hands.

"During debriefing, the medic repeated the business about Hugh killing your parents. John didn't mention it. It's unlike him to filter information, but perhaps he felt he was protecting your integrity. Which proves again how dangerous it is for field operatives to form attachments.

"In any event, I realized that last night's operation had somehow touched memories from almost thirty years ago. Sooner or later, you'd realize that it was not Hugh but William you remembered. I decided it was in the organization's best interest to bring you face-to-face with him, give you a little guidance, show you what actually happened."

"Guidance?" I lifted a fingertip in the direction of the IV. "Bastard."

Mac stiffened his back, lifted his chin. He stared at me, lips pursed, frowning, clearly offended.

"I have *never* set out to do you harm, Jane."

Body language signaled that his declaration was spontaneous, heartfelt. He leaned toward me, shoulders shifting toward his spine, fingers splaying slightly in my direction. As he spoke, he lifted his eyebrows, moved his head fractionally— left, right, left.

Subtle stuff.

I lifted my left hand a half inch off the mattress, kept the palm turned toward me, ignored the tug of the IV needle as I raised my middle finger. My declaration was also spontaneous and heartfelt. Unlike Mac's, it was honest.

He got the message, retreated to his pipe. He stabbed at the burned tobacco with a pipe nail, tapped out the contents of the bowl, restuffed it with fresh tobacco. He took his time. When he looked at me again, his jaw was relaxed, his voice conciliatory.

"I've regretted that day for a long time. The situation just, well, went out of control. But try to understand our frustration. The only witness to a triple homicide was a little girl with no memory of the incident. And the drugs we had then . . ."

Mac's eyes darted to the bag of saline solution hanging from the IV stand. He cleared his throat, took a drag on his pipe, continued talking.

"Suffice to say, one couldn't use such drugs on a child. We hoped that, under questioning, you'd give us *something*. Instead, we compounded your trauma. When William pulled you from under that table . . . I carried you to the infirmary, Jane. You lay in my arms, clammy and unresponsive. I was afraid that your mind . . . But within a few hours, you'd snapped out of it and seemed quite normal. Except that your memory loss had extended to include much of the interrogation, too."

"You didn't hesitate to use drugs today. Why not ask what happened the day my parents were killed?"

"Because anything you remembered would be irrelevant."

He lifted a hand to stop my objection and continued speaking.

"Not to you, perhaps. But certainly to anyone else. I'm sorry, but *assuming* you saw anything, how would we pursue it?

The incident is decades in the past. It took place on foreign soil. And accusations based solely on recovered memory are rarely taken seriously. Either here or in Greece."

I didn't like it, but he made sense. That left only one reason for today's session. Anger flared again.

"You dragged me through hell to *protect* Sir William?"

Mac nodded.

"And you. I feared you would seek revenge unless you were convinced of his innocence. And I can't have that, Jane. Not twice. This time, I would have been compelled to protect an important ally."

I should have been shocked that he would speak so casually of ordering my death. I wasn't. It was self-deception to believe that anything more than duty drove our relationship. And, in fact, I felt more betrayed by his use of drugs than by his willingness to kill me.

"Why not just tell me he was innocent?"

He stared down at his pipe, puffed out his cheeks and lips as he exhaled, then lifted his eyes to mine.

"Would you have believed me, Jane?"

He already knew the answer.

I replied anyway, anger gone, my regret mirroring his.

"No, I wouldn't have. You taught me better than that."

12

For two days, I tossed and turned, shivered and perspired.

Two days of infection and fever, of drug reaction.

Two days. Flashbacks assaulted reality. Nightmares fragmented the boundary between waking and sleeping. Hands crept from beneath the bed, grabbed my ankles. Alex held me, kept me safe. Red gelatin cooled my throat. Kitty-mou slept on my pillow. John's voice. Brian's gentle touch. Lovely Lady Jane. Sips of warm soup. Mac calling my name. Twin coffins. Bloody bodies. You weren't supposed to be here. Greek curses. Clawing branches. Yellow eyes. Yellow eyes. Yellow eyes.

Then the fever broke, left me weak, aching. And lucid.

I ate.

I slept.

I rested.

I recovered.

A few days later, I sat on the edge of my bed, fully dressed, my IV removed only because I'd threatened to remove it myself.

My head throbbed an interesting counterpoint to my throbbing arm.

I was leaving. Against doctor's orders, which was easy. More difficult to get beyond the electric fence topped by razor wire and the armed guards who patrolled the perimeter. Almost impossible to arrange transportation from the remote location. I needed a car and, for safety's sake, a driver.

Bottom line, I needed Mac's permission to leave.

I lifted the phone, dialed his number, got Miss Marston. I said good morning and asked for Mac. Please.

She was cool, polite, and clearly had no intention of letting him know I was on the phone.

"I'm sorry. He's reading the mail. I'll let him know you called and have him ring you back when it's convenient."

I wasn't waiting. I gave up on civility and simply pulled rank, rattling off a formula that assured immediate access. Day or night.

"Now," I added. "Or it'll be your job."

A click, a pause, and then Mac was on the line.

"Hello, Jane. How are you?"

"Well enough to leave here."

"I think you're being premature. I just talked with Dr. Bowers. She recommended against releasing you. And you know that it's always inadvisable for operatives to leave before they're fully fit. I'd suggest you spend some time using the facilities."

The clinic housed a full gym, a swimming pool, and a shooting range. And even midwinter drizzle failed to diminish the beauty of its grounds—walking paths, park benches, manicured lawns and low hedgerows. But I still felt more an inmate than a patient.

I shook my head. Pointless, because Mac couldn't see me. Foolish, because it worsened my headache.

"I'm fit enough to return to my flat," I said. "I doubt that any of my neighbors will attack me. And I promise to stay out of the pubs. Please, Mac. Don't force me to break out of here and hitchhike back to London."

I didn't have to thumb a ride.

I was home by mid-afternoon and immediately noticed two things.

The message light on my answering machine was flashing—someone had called my unlisted number. My telltales were disturbed—someone had been in my flat.

Awkwardly, I used my left hand to take my automatic from the webbing holster beneath my left arm. Then I walked through my flat, checking every room. No one was there.

Which left the question, who *had* been there?

I thought about it as I hit the button on the answering machine. A moment later, Joey's voice had my complete attention.

"Jane. It's December twenty-ninth. Around eight A.M. I thought maybe you'd be home. Tommy gave me your number. Alex doesn't know I have it. There's a problem here. Please call me back at home. Or the office." She rattled off both phone numbers, complete with area codes.

The next message was from Joey, too. It had been left earlier this morning.

"It's Joey again. Maybe you're out of town. Otherwise, I'm sure you would have called. Tommy says I shouldn't keep bothering you. But I know you care about Alex. Please, please call me."

I hit the Erase button, consulted the clock and dialed the real estate office she owned as I swallowed against the cold lump of fear that made my throat ache. A month had passed since I'd left Savannah. A month without phone calls. This certainly wasn't mere matchmaking on Joey's part. But in a real emergency, Tommy would have made the call himself.

I got *her* answering machine, cursed under my breath. Where the hell was she?

Emergency room, I thought immediately. Then I told myself I was being stupid. She was probably with a client. I spoke to her machine.

"Jane, here. Sorry I didn't call sooner. I've been on holiday and just received your message. I'll wait here until I hear from you."

Then I dialed her home number and left the same message.

I hung up, then stood for a moment staring at the phone and feeling anxious. A waste of time. I refocused on my intruder problem.

I fixed myself a pot of tea, pulled a chair up to the window, rested my aching head on a pillow, waited for the phone to ring, and watched the world go by. Watched for patterns of movement on the busy sidewalk four stories below. Watched for odd breaks in those patterns.

Two hours later, the phone hadn't rung. But I'd picked out the spotters among the pedestrians and was willing to lay odds that Mac had ordered my flat transformed into a first-class fishbowl. Time to test the theory.

I went into the living room, walked over to the fireplace, put my foot against the cast-iron set of tools, and sent them crashing against the stone hearth. I cried out. Then I waited.

Within minutes, footsteps pounded up the steps.

I opened the door before they broke it down.

They stood, weapons in hand, shaking with exertion and adrenaline. A male. A female. Both dressed in black and neon.

Both with pale, narrow faces topped by short, spiky hair. Multiple silver rings through both pairs of ears, an eyebrow, and one nostril. In London, the look was as unremarkable as city suits. Or blue jeans. And the point was to blend with the environment.

Neither operative was a day over twenty-five.

I doubted they were happy about baby-sitting.

I tried to remember how young I had once been.

"The trick is to focus on the sequence, to keep the sounds in context," I said mildly.

He looked at his feet, murmured, "Sorry."

She met my eyes.

"You might try being more careful, what with your injury and all."

Nothing solicitous about her tone.

She'd last longer.

Joey called just after ten.

I wasn't asleep.

"Alex's acting peculiar," she said. "You know he doesn't scare easily. But something's definitely scaring him. I'm sure of it. So is Tommy. But he won't talk to either of us."

I leaned back in my chair, pressed my eyes shut, wondered why I'd returned her call. What exactly do you want me to do? I thought. Catch a plane to Savannah? Bang on Alex's door? Say, 'So sorry that I left and all that, but here I am. Tell me what's troubling you?'

Essentially, that was what she wanted.

I shook my head. Same result as earlier that day. Pain.

"Alex has a lot of sense, Joey. He'll ask for help when—and if—he needs it. And he'll go to you or Tommy. I assure you, he won't call me."

"But, Jane—"

"No."

"At least phone him? Would you do that much? For me?"

Anything to make her go away.

"I'll think about it," I said. And hung up.

I popped an antibiotic tablet and a couple more pain pills, accessorized a biceps' worth of gauze bandage with sweatpants and a large T-shirt, and crawled into bed.

I slept.

Kitty-mou was crying.

With eyes still closed, I groped through the bedding, searching for her. She'd been tucked in beside me, curled into the warmth of my stomach when I'd fallen asleep. And now . . .

I sat up in bed, wide-eyed, suddenly awake.

She was gone. Out of my bed, out of my bedroom. Grandpa's Christmas gift to me. I'd had her less than a day, and I'd already lost her.

I slipped my legs from beneath the eiderdown's warmth, shivering despite the long flannel nightgown I wore. I reached for the quilted robe at the end of my bed, pulled it on. I hated the cold, damp weather, hated England. Greece was bright and warm, our home a swirl of color enclosed by whitewashed walls. The stone walls of Grandpa's house enclosed only chill and shadows.

Kitty-mou called again, her piteous cry muffled by the closed bedroom door. I rushed across the room, pulled open the door, stepped into the hallway. No kitten.

I stood very still, listening. Mewing echoed upward from the first floor. I ran barefoot down the staircase and across the entry hall, following the sound. It stayed always ahead of me.

The mewing stopped abruptly as I reached the Great Hall's massive oak doors. They stood slightly ajar, so I slipped through the narrow opening and stood staring into the darkness beyond, trying to match the lurking forms with my memory of the room's interior.

Earlier, Christmas festivities had banished the shadows. The Great Hall was alive with music and laughter and the warm, friendly smells of apples and cinnamon and oranges. At the center of the hall, the Christmas tree, taller than some of the houses in the village, had twinkled with fairy lights.

Now the stone floors were cold, the fire in the central hearth burned down to embers. The Christmas tree loomed dark and silent, stripped of its brightly wrapped packages, stripped of its reason for being.

Kitty-mou called again. She was in the tree. Ignoring the icy stone floor and the shadows snatching at the hem of my robe, I ran to it. Clutching my robe close to my body, I peered up into the branches.

One by one, the fairy lights glowed on. Red, green, blue. White, yellow, red. Tinsel garlands, stirred by some unfelt breeze, swayed gently from the tips of the branches, reflecting the lights. The longer I stared, the brighter the tree became.

Still, I couldn't see Kitty-mou.

I went down on my hands and knees, crawled beneath the tree and stared upward along its massive trunk, up through the branches, past rigid tin soldiers, fragile glass ornaments and tiny straw horses.

The star at the top of the tree burst into flames.

The fire spread, moving steadily down the tree.

Heat twisted the branches into skeletal fingers. The straw horses smoldered, blackened. The tin soldiers melted, dripped scalding grey liquid onto my skin. The ornaments exploded, peppering me with glass.

I covered my head with my arms, huddled beneath the tree, terrified. But I didn't run away. Not this time.

Kitty-mou screamed. I looked up. She was there, out of reach, clinging to the tree trunk.

I slipped out of my robe, held it outstretched.

"Jump!"

She did as I said, came crashing through the fiery branches, landed in the center of my robe. Quickly, I folded it around her.

The smell of petrol hung in the air.

Thick, oily smoke stung my eyes and made breathing difficult.

The tree exploded.

Heat and flames consumed the room.

Heat.

Flames.

I sat bolt upright, wrenched from sleep.

And inhaled smoke.

Coughing, gagging, I kicked away the bedding and rolled to the floor.

Down low, there was air that could be breathed.

I did just that as I surveyed the room.

Dark, thick smoke. Flames boiling up my bedroom wall. The wall with three doors on it. Hallway. Closet. Bathroom. Escape in that direction was impossible.

I yelled for help just once, hoping that Mac's people were listening. Then I crawled toward the window.

The pall of smoke descended, eating up the oxygen near the floor.

Tears streamed down my face. My nostrils and throat burned. My ears were filled with the roaring of the flames. I choked. I wheezed. I fought for every breath.

Finally, I reached the window and opened it. A moment's relief, a gulp of cold night air, and then the smoke followed me, wrapping itself around me, unwilling to let me go.

I didn't panic.

I'd chosen my flat with escape in mind.

Decorative brickwork on the face of the building incorporated a four-inch-wide ledge that ran past the bedroom window. Ten meters along the ledge to an ancient copper drainpipe at the corner of the building, and I could climb down from my tower.

With my back to the street, I scooted out onto the sill and grabbed the exterior window frame to pull myself to my feet. A bolt of agony tore through my right arm, punctuating a shattering truth. I didn't have two strong arms. I couldn't climb down without them.

I wouldn't survive if I stayed where I was.

Using my left hand for support, I stood, reestablished my balance, then faced outward. I let go of the window frame and moved sideways, keeping my head, heels, shoulders, and spine in contact with the building. Palms flat against the brick and fingers splayed, I edged away from the heat and smoke pouring from the open window.

I yelled, "Fire!" and "Help!" and "Hurry!"

Lights came on.

A dog began barking.

Shouts came from the street below.
Soon, sirens wailed in the distance.
I hung on.
I waited.
I asked myself if I believed in coincidence.

13

I stood in the midst of the fire trucks and the ambulances and the crowds and the refugees from my building.

No sign of Mac's people.

Lots of talk of arson.

Cops and firemen trolled the crowd, seeking information.

I avoided them, kept my questions to myself.

I didn't, in fact, believe in coincidence.

I did believe in betrayal.

I slipped away from the scene. I kept the fire department's blanket around my shoulders, lifted a wallet from an ambulance attendant and another from one of the cops, and walked around a corner.

Signs at the intersections, installed for tourists who drove on the wrong side of the road, warned, "Look Right." I did. Right, then left. Forward and back. I made sure I wasn't followed.

A few corners later, I dropped the wallets minus their cash and credit cards into a post box and went to the nearest tube station. I spent a few minutes in the public washroom, washed smoke streaks from my face and combed my hair with my fingers. Then I took the Underground in an area where no one cared if I wore baggy sweatpants and no shoes and wrapped myself in a blanket.

The hotel took cash. A handful of stolen pounds bought me a shared bath that reeked of vomit and mildew, a pay phone in the hallway, and a bed too filthy to sleep in. I slept for a few hours, sitting on the floor with my back against the door and my blanket wrapped around me.

I dreamt that a rat was chewing on my right arm.

At about four A.M., when even the prostitutes and their drunken johns had stopped crashing through the hallway, I woke up and phoned Mac's private number.

He didn't sound as if he'd been sleeping.

"Where are you?" he said immediately.

"Somewhere safe. Where were your people?"

"They were arrested on suspicion of selling drugs. Someone called the Met and reported them. Anonymously, of course."

Interesting timing.

"Who's trying to kill me, Mac?"

Silence.

"Who are you trying to trap?"

More silence.

I made a guess, based on the events of the past week.

"Sir William?"

Finally, I received an answer of sorts.

"Perhaps. I can't be positive. He did seem disturbed after meeting you. As a matter of fact, he stopped by my office."

Mac stopped speaking.

Games. I was tempted to hang up. Instead, I took a firm grip on my patience and kept my voice even.

"Why?"

"He wanted to be sure you understood he was innocent of any wrongdoing. I reassured him and thanked him for his cooperation the other night. I told him how pleased I was that your memory was finally returning. It's so much healthier, you know, not to repress things."

"You set me up," I said flatly.

"Yes."

It would have been easier to hate him if he'd denied it.

"And you told him where I lived?"

John and Mac had that information, as did Alex and Tommy. Miss Marston had access to it, too. Beyond that, I could think of no one else.

"Your file may have been compromised. Miss Marston did have to call me away for a minor emergency. William was alone in my office for quite some time, and your file was on my desk."

A woman's shriek interrupted us. The sound came from a nearby room and was followed immediately by deeper, male tones. His words were indecipherable. I tensed, ready to run. But the noise resolved itself into nothing more threatening than enthusiastic sex.

I fed more coins into the phone.

"You might have warned me, waited until I could defend myself."

Mac managed to sound offended.

"I wasn't certain that William would attack you, and I'm not fully convinced that *he* was behind the fire. And, if you'll recall, I *did* ask you to stay at the clinic until you were better recovered. When you refused, despite short notice and personnel shortages, I assigned operatives to protect you."

"Incompetent children. Damn it, Mac. I nearly *died* in that fire."

Beyond that, I'd lost a precious possession. My furniture and clothing could be replaced, and a trip to my grandfather's estate—mine now—would yield duplicate photos of my parents. But I'd had only one photo of Brian. Framed. On my bedroom wall. It was gone forever. I thought of the silver menagerie given to me by Mac and found comfort in imagining it reduced to shapeless blobs of metal.

"*Did* Sir William murder my parents?" I asked.

"I wasn't there. How could I know?"

"You'll know with certainty if he kills me?"

He actually chuckled.

"That's a bit extreme. We'll know when, and if, he *attempts* to kill you."

I tucked the phone between ear and shoulder, rubbed my aching arm, pushed away thoughts of sleep, and wondered about hidden agendas instead.

"So, you've set your trap," I said. "The question becomes, why the hell should I cooperate? I can disappear. Go so deep you'll never find me. And neither will your killer. Whoever he is."

"If it is Sir William, I should think you'd want justice."

"You mean revenge. As long as it looks like self-defense."

Months earlier, he'd told me revenge was dangerous and morally indefensible. Now, apparently, it suited his purposes.

Mac coughed and cleared his throat.

"Go somewhere safe, Jane, and recover properly. I'd suggest the clinic, but the choice is yours. No matter where you go, William will be told that you've returned to the clinic to receive treatment for something credible—perhaps burns, or pneumonia. Council and Jacoby are near the end of an operation. I think you'll agree that *they* are competent. When you return, I'll assign them to help protect you from person or persons unknown."

My instinct was to tell him no, to escape his endless manipulation any way I could. But I knew I was too exhausted and in too much pain to make a wise decision. I needed a safe place to rest. I needed to consider my options. I needed, most of all, to remember what had happened that day in Greece. If not to avenge my parents, certainly for my own protection.

I doubted I could remember on my own, but I didn't trust Mac enough to return to the clinic.

I asked myself who I *did* trust.

One name, one face, came to mind.

"Is Savannah still secure? Did you give Sir William that information, too?"

"William knows nothing about your life there. I give you my word, Janie."

I believed him only because I could think of no reason for him to lie.

"I'll call you," I said. "In a few weeks."

"Very well." He paused, then added an unexpected postscript. "Sometimes, Janie, you remind me of your mother. I was very fond of her, you know."

He hung up.

I stood for a moment, phone in hand, attempting to define undefinable feelings. How should I feel, I wondered, about parents I hardly knew?

The woman in the nearby room shrieked her way to climax.

Moments later, in the midst of sudden quiet, I called Alex collect.

He accepted the charges.

He didn't ask why.

For a few minutes, conversation flowed easily as polite adults expressed polite interest in safe topics. We made formula inquiries about each other's health and gave each other formula answers. Alex asked about the weather in London, then told me there'd been a cold snap in Savannah. The temperature had dropped below freezing for the past two weeks, but now it was raining and 65 degrees.

Silence after that—a crystal-clear, hear-a-pin-drop silence.

I found myself wishing for the days before communications satellites, when distance was filled with the ever-shifting crackle and drone of a transatlantic cable connection.

Then Alex stepped into the silence with a question that told me he'd been listening to more than my words.

"Are you all right, Jane? You sound—"

A pause, and I could imagine him standing in his cheery kitchen, leaning his tall frame back against the kitchen counter—dark eyes troubled, generous mouth pulled down into a frown, handsome features tense with the effort of balancing his intuitions against my need for privacy.

"—you sound as if you're hurting."

Hurting. Like many Americans, Alex used the word to imply emotional pain.

As always, his perceptions frightened me, left me feeling stripped and vulnerable. My impulse was to protect myself with a lie. I didn't.

"I need a place to stay, Alex. Somewhere safe. And I need your help."

More silence, during which I feared he might not issue the invitation I had no right to ask for.

I needn't have worried.

His voice was half an octave deeper when he spoke.

I blamed the slight tremor I heard on the connection.

"Come on home, Jane."

I assumed that my bank accounts and credit cards were flagged and that Sir William would find out about charges or money withdrawals. My passport, credit cards, and IDs were smoldering in the ashes in my flat, as was the key to the safe-deposit box containing papers and plastic issued to one of my alter egos, Jan Nixon. I sighed, told myself that it was a poor backup plan that didn't account for a devastating fire, and then used my job skills.

I left my door open a crack, waited until I heard a door open, and then staggered into the hallway, toward the bathroom. Along the way, I watched to see which door had opened. Twice I discovered that the john was leaving, but the prostitute had remained behind. Third time lucky. My noisy neighbor and her male companion left together and left their room unoccupied.

I used a discarded hairpin as a picklock on the room's worn and battered mechanism. Even left-handed, it was easy. Inside, the closet yielded an empty purse, a dress whose fit bordered on the obscene, a woolly jumper, and a pair of shoes a half size too small.

I left the hotel and joined the crush of commuters on the Underground. On New Year's Eve day, the crowd included a large number of holiday shoppers, which made my work easier. I started on the East London line, transferred to the District line, then spent another hour or two on the Picadilly line. The resulting cash and credit cards bought me a passport with my picture and someone else's name on it, a night in a hotel room with bath and without roaches, clothing and luggage, and indirect transportation to Savannah.

14

"Bait."

"Ma'am?"

The cabby glanced over his shoulder into the backseat. Wiry-thin and dark-skinned, he was old enough to have children who remembered signs on restroom doors specifying sex *and* color.

He had, in fact, just finished telling me that he had six children, if you counted the two who had died. Which he did. 'Cause almighty God cared for *His* children from before the cradle to after the grave, and didn't that mean that a man was obliged to do the same? For his children and all fourteen of his grandchildren. Not to mention his five great-grandchildren. I'd murmured something about the importance of duty, and he'd nodded.

I leaned forward in the seat, pointed past him to a dilapidated building down the road.

"Just reading aloud," I said.

WILLIE'S BAIT.

The red block letters were peeling and faded, as were the smaller letters and crude illustrations that added specifics. CRICKETS. SHINERS. WORMS. SHRIMP. And then, beneath that, in paint not quite as peeled or faded, the words PEACH PRE-SERVES & FRESH PRODUCE.

The taxi ride had taken me south from the airport, along Dean Forest Road and then farther south along the Atlantic Coast Highway. From there, we'd swung eastward, past a grove of pecan trees and along a familiar flat stretch of narrow road bordered by a wooded marsh. And then past the bait shop. Though I'd often traveled the route, the old building had always been covered by kudzu. But frost had reduced the relentless vine to ropy stalks and limp grey-brown leaves. Through it, the sign painted on the west wall was readable.

As the taxi drew nearer the bait shop, I picked out other features. The corrugated metal roof extended beyond the face of the building, shading a sagging porch. A single step, dark with rot, led up onto that porch. The doorway into the shop was boarded over with mismatched planks. Narrow window frames, glassless and gaping, flanked the entrance.

During the growing season, the kudzu had groped its way in through the windows and out through holes in the roof. The vine covered the porch and the rooftop, hung like a tattered curtain between the shop and the skeletal remains of several oak trees. It blocked the entrance to the tiny parking area, imprisoning an old car and a corroding propane tank in thick brown cords.

The cabby shook his grizzled head and chuckled as we drove past.

"Times sure do change. Back in 'forty, the gov'ment paid my daddy eight dollars an acre to plant it. Called it the miracle vine. Now they callin' it the vine that ate the South, keep searchin' for ways to kill it."

Just past the bait shop, the road curved sharply, then straightened to bridge the Ogeechee River with a long, flat span bordered by wooden railings. Alex had once told me that a trail bounded the river, crossed a section of old plantation rice fields, and intersected a path through the densely wooded area at the back of his property. A shortcut, he had called it. Only half a mile. Then he'd described the mud, mosquitoes, snakes, and alligators he'd encountered over the years. The road was far less direct, but drier. From the bridge, it wound for another couple miles before reaching the lane leading to Alex's house.

Halfway across the bridge, the cab slowed. Below us, the river was high and fast. Normally, waist-high marsh grass covered the shallow riverbank, making it impossible to see exactly where land ended and river began. Now, only the tallest fronds were visible above the water.

The cabby's cocoa brown eyes met my hazel ones in the rearview mirror.

"Folks 'round here say Willie's ghost fishes off this very bridge. They all talk about seein' him—fishin' pole, bait bucket, and all. Willie's been seen so often that last Halloween the paper wrote about the haunting."

A story I'd apparently missed.

His eyes returned to the road as he stepped on the accelerator, but he kept talking.

"Been maybe two years, now. Willie liked his likker. Prob'ly got drunk and fell in. Leastways, that's what some think. 'Course, other folks, they all say it wasn't by accident. Rumor is, Willie got hisself mixed up with the kind of fellas a smart man don't get mixed up with. Problem is, folks can pretty much speculate either way."

We were well past the bridge when he glanced in the rearview mirror again, probably wanting to be sure he still had an audience.

He did.

"Cain't even be real sure the body the police found was Willie's. Cooters and crabs didn't leave much. I, for one, figure it *was* him. Mostly 'cause life kinda works that way. Willie, he got bait from the river all his life. Then he end up being nothing but river bait hisself."

Bait, I thought, and shuddered. I vowed that if I ever agreed to serve as bait for Mac's trap, I would fare better than Willie.

Twin stone pillars marked the entrance to the Callaghan property and the end of the blacktop road. The road continued on as little more than a mile-long muddy track that ended at an eroding boat ramp providing public access to the river.

Ten-foot-tall wrought-iron gates, rusted open for at least a generation, hung from the pillars. The driver swung his cab between them, slowed to accommodate the pecan-shell surface of the narrow lane. We drove half a mile through wooded marsh. Then the lane straightened. The cabby's whistle was long and low when he saw the white, two-story plantation home at the top of a gentle rise. Doric columns supported the verandah and balcony. Wide steps swept up between the two center columns.

"Nice place. Belongs to the police chief, don't it? You a friend of his? Visiting for long?"

"A friend, yes," I said. "And probably not."

A circular drive looped in front of the house, past a carport, then back to the lane. From the carport, a flagstone path led to the fenced kitchen garden behind the house.

I leaned forward, looked down the driveway, checking to see

which cars were in the carport. As usual, Alex's personal cars were parked side by side in the shelter. One was a newer, white sedan of the type that screamed "unmarked police car" to most urban American teenagers. The other was a boxy 1969 Chevy Blazer in once-white over faded blue, with dark red spots of primer around the mirror mounts, wheel wells, and gas cap. The back half of the truck was filled with fishing gear. According to Alex, it was the 167th Blazer ever manufactured. He'd told me that proudly. A good reason *not* to own it, I thought. But I hadn't expressed that opinion or asked about gas mileage.

Judging from the mud spattering and thickly caked tires, the two vehicles parked beside the carport had served as the day's transportation. The bright red pickup truck was Tommy's. And the squad car—white, with red-and-blue pinstripes running its length and POLICE spelled out in blue block letters on its side panels—had probably been driven by Alex.

I glanced at my watch. It was after five. I wondered whether Alex and Tommy were taking a dinner break or were off duty. Either way, they weren't there to greet *me*. When I'd talked to Alex, I'd been vague about my arrival.

The cab rolled to a stop near the front door. I opened my bag, caught a whiff of new leather, paid my fare. The cabby carried my bags to the top of the steps.

As he walked back to his cab, I stood on the verandah, looking out at the wide-branched oaks that dwarfed the massive house, watching the grey-green moss sway in the wind.

Pretty. Like tinsel on a Christmas tree. Until the flames scorched the branches and the ornaments began falling, shattering—

For much of my life, I'd ignored the flashbacks and the nightmares. They were irrelevant, distracting. They hurt. And since the drug session at the clinic, they'd become more frequent, more vivid, more painful. My habit was to interrupt the flood of images, to refocus on something—anything—else. But now I fought that instinct and scrutinized the odd, subconscious associations. I saw—

Twisted olive branches. Thick, black smoke boiling up into a clear, blue sky. Shards of metal raining down on me. Something heavy hitting the ground. A polished black boot, laces neatly tied, a bloody—

And then I was back, standing on the verandah, the face of the elderly black driver looking up at me through the open window of the cab. He was speaking.

I forced myself to concentrate on his words.

"You take care, ma'am."

Then he repeated the words, saying them more slowly, as if delivering a different, more important message.

"You take care."

He drove away.

I left my suitcases where they were, lifted the slim canvas bag containing my new laptop. The old one had burned along with the backup discs and the hard copy. I would have to re-create the chapters I'd written. Not tragic, but annoying.

I slipped the laptop's broad strap over my shoulder, crossed the verandah to the front door. I put my hand on the ornate knob, intending to let myself into the house. Despite his position as Savannah's chief of police—or, perhaps, because of it—Alex was the least security-conscious person I knew. Except during a brief period when I'd first stayed with him, Alex rarely locked his doors. He'd once told me that he was demonstrating his confidence in the city's police force. I'd suggested that he was simply too lazy to bother with keys.

To my surprise, the front door was locked.

I walked down the length of the verandah to the left of the entrance, tried the two sets of French doors that opened out from the suite I'd occupied before I'd tucked into Alex's bedroom. Locked. I went to the opposite end of the verandah. French doors opened out from the living room and the den. They, too, were locked.

Odd, but no real problem.

Except that I no longer had a house key.

I lifted my finger to the bell, then hesitated as I remembered that, almost a year earlier, Alex had shown me where he kept a spare key. I told myself he would certainly have moved it. I checked beneath a nearby flowerpot, anyway, and found it there.

I let myself in, pausing to check the remote arming station on the foyer wall. The alarm was on. I took a moment to recall the code, tapped it into the keypad, then rearmed the device.

Curious. The alarm was rarely used.

Alex had installed it for my safety before he'd discovered that I could take care of myself. The last time he'd suggested arming it, I'd taken him around to the utility box on the side of the house, pointed to the modular interface between the alarm system and the telephone line, used a screwdriver and demonstrated how easily the alarm could be *disarmed*. After that, he'd seemed content to resume his old, sloppy habits.

Joey was right, I thought. Something had scared him.

I put the laptop and my purse down beside the oak coat tree, peeled off the loose jacket that hid my bandages, and hung it on one of the curved branches. Two branches were already filled. A bulky nylon jacket hung from one. It was indigo, with the bright SPD logo on the left breast. Hanging opposite the jacket was a full-length yellow slicker with SPD in large, reflective letters on its back. Absentmindedly, I reached down to tap the handle of a malacca walking stick poking out from the umbrella stand near the hall tree. The L-shaped handle was of yellowing ivory, bound with a tarnished filigreed band, carved to resemble a serpent's head.

"For luck," Alex had explained when I'd first seen him perform the quick ritual. "This belonged to my father's great-granddaddy, who built this house."

I crossed the spacious entry hall. Overhead, ceiling fans spun quietly, pushing warm air downward from the twelve-foot ceilings. Except for the kitchen, the first-floor rooms had glossy, dark wood floors and dark cherry wood paneling. It was potentially oppressive, but light-colored area rugs, fanciful pieces of art glass, and the clutter of everyday living kept the huge rooms homey.

To my left, through a set of double pocket doors, was a two-room suite—a library, a guest bedroom, and a bathroom. To my right, another set of pocket doors opened into the living room. Beyond that was the den. A formal and seldom used dining room adjoined the living room and shared the north end of the first floor with the eat-in kitchen.

In front of me, a wide staircase with ornate spindles and polished handrails on both sides swept up to the open second-floor landing.

The wide second-floor hallway—blessedly devoid of family portraits—branched east and west. Four rooms, rarely used, shared the east side of the house. In the west wing, the two front-facing bedrooms had been combined into Alex's living area; the two guest rooms opposite overlooked the well-kept backyard. A small back stairwell led from the second floor back down to the kitchen.

The kitchen was the least secure room in a house that seemed to have been designed with a total disregard for security. The back door had a large window set into its upper half.

Interior French doors connected the kitchen to a bright, window-lined solarium. A narrow, white-enameled door opened down to a shelf-lined cellar, which had a trapdoor that opened up into the backyard. A glossy mahogany swinging door led into the dining room.

The main entrance to the kitchen was tucked into the shadow of the formal staircase. That door was rarely closed. I paused within a few feet of it, listening more closely to the sounds drifting from the kitchen. A bright jazz tune—mostly trumpet and piano—was playing on the radio. Tommy was laughing. And then Alex spoke.

God! how much I'd missed his voice, the way it smoothed to a deep, caressing murmur, the way his hands . . .

I shook my head and banished lust by thinking about Sir William.

15

Neither Tommy nor Alex noticed me come into the kitchen.

They sat with their backs to me, the tails of their indigo uniform shirts pulled from the waists of matching trousers, their booted feet resting on the kitchen table.

The table was not a pretty sight. Though an effort had been made to tie it into the bright decor of the kitchen, it was an odd note in the plantation home. Too new to be antique, too old to be modern, the table was ugly enough to be retro. Of 1950s vintage, its Formica surface was swirled with intertwining layers of grey and red and silvery white. Originally bright chrome and gloss, the top was scratched, the chrome trim and legs worn.

The chrome and color was repeated on the four kitchen chairs.

At the moment, two of those chairs were tipped back at dangerous angles. Between the chairs on which Alex and Tommy sat so precariously was a third. It was pushed slightly back from a corner of the table, its tubular metal legs solidly on the floor, its vinyl seat and back concealed by an open carry-out pizza box. The fourth chair was tucked into the table. Tommy's SPD jacket was draped over its back.

The wastebasket had been moved from its spot beneath the sink to the middle of the kitchen. Around it, the floor was littered with crushed beer cans.

"It's weird, man. That's what it is. Weird," Tommy was saying. "And dangerous. Night-of-the-living-dead stuff."

Alex laughed.

"As your oldest buddy, I'm obliged to tell you that you're suffering from an acute case of fatherhood complicated by cable television. You and the boys have spent too many nights watching *Nightmare on Elm Street* reruns over beer and baby food."

"No way. Those movies scare the shit out of me. And I sure as hell wouldn't let my babies watch them. Besides, what you saw was *not* imagination."

"I think I'm probably the best judge of what I saw. It wasn't real."

"Then why are you telling me about these *hallucinations* of yours?"

Unmistakable tension in Tommy's voice.

Alex ran a hand through his hair, sighed.

"Figured it was only fair," he said casually. "You bein' my second in command and all, *Lieutenant* Grayson."

The reminder of his recent promotion seemed to spur Tommy's anger.

"And you want me to do *exactly what* with this information? Wait around until you're some kind of fucking statistic for the violent-crimes unit?"

For a moment, the room was silent.

"I want you to worry, 'cause that's what you do best," Alex said.

There was anger in his voice, too.

"Wouldn't have to worry if you'd keep your white ass out of trouble," Tommy muttered.

"Yeah . . . Well . . . So's your old man. *And* your mama wears combat boots."

Tommy's irritation dissolved into laughter.

"You're hopeless, man. Fucking hopeless."

He picked up his can of beer, his hand large enough to completely conceal the red and white label. The can was halfway to his mouth when he paused.

"Hey, I almost forgot. Miz Briggs called me today."

"Lady seems real fond of you. Space invaders again? I thought her daughter-in-law was seeing to it that she took her medication."

"I think she is. Miz Briggs hasn't called for months. And she wasn't calling about ET. Seems she was out walking her dog last night and saw Willie. Gave him five dollars to come by and mend her screens. Like he used to. He didn't show up this morning, and she was pissed. Which was why she called me. She said she wanted me to drive over to his place and haul his lazy bones out of bed."

"You tell her he was dead?"

"Sure did. She said in that case, he'd stolen her money, and she wanted to file a formal complaint. I gave her five dollars and told her not to be paying for work in advance."

Alex nodded.

"Good solution. Reimburse yourself out of petty cash, okay?"

Then Alex tipped his beer can to his lips, took a long sip, and turned the can upside down. No liquid spilled out.

"You ready?"

"Wait a sec."

Tommy finished his beer.

"Ready."

They began counting. On five, each man crushed the can he held and threw it overhand. Both cans landed in the wastebasket. Tommy and Alex belched in unison.

I burst out laughing.

Two sets of chair legs crashed squarely onto the floor, immediately followed by two pairs of boots. Heads turned, and startled eyes looked in my direction.

"Don't get up," I said quickly. "I want to fix this scene in my memory."

I crossed the kitchen, leaned over, and touched my lips to the fine, white scar that slanted above Alex's right eyebrow.

"Hello, love," I said. "Happy New Year."

It was January second.

"Hello, Jane."

His voice was cool, polite. Not quite hostile.

He made no move to touch me.

Three days between his invitation and my arrival. He'd had three days to recall that in our brief history together, I'd deceived him, manipulated him, used him, and walked out on him. It was no surprise that he was unenthusiastic about volunteering for more betrayal.

Tommy's chair scraped across the floor. He stood, waved vaguely in the direction of the clock above the sink, and snatched up his jacket.

No smile on his face, either.

I'd abandoned his friend. But as far as Tommy knew, I'd come back to help at Joey's request. Awkward for him.

"Welcome back, Jane. Sorry, but I've gotta run. Ginnie's waiting dinner on me."

I glanced at the open pizza box, saw three small squares of pizza in the middle of a much larger grease-marked circle, and hoped that Ginnie hadn't gone to too much trouble.

Tommy left through the back door, which was apparently off the alarm circuit. And then Alex and I were alone. I sat down in the chair Tommy had vacated, leaving a chair and the remains of the pizza between us.

Alex picked up another can of beer. Instead of opening it, he examined its label, an activity that apparently required all his attention.

"How was your flight?" he said, not looking up.

"Ill-advised, apparently. You invited *me* back. But based on this reception, I assume you've changed your mind."

He put the beer can down, turned his head, met my eyes.

"You'll leave me again."

A statement. No doubt in his voice. No self-pity, either. The lines around his mouth were hard and angry, the hurt in his eyes difficult to miss. He was protecting himself. From me.

I considered how I could overcome his defenses, sought the most effective way to get what I wanted. The truth, I thought suddenly. He would help me if I told him the truth.

I nodded and matched my tone to his.

"Probably."

"Then why come back at all? And don't give me that crap about needing a safe place to stay." He lifted his chin, indicated my injured arm. "I won't even ask how that happened. But I'm sure MI-5 has a marvelous health plan and lots of nice, secure places to send damaged agents."

I picked my way carefully through unfamiliar territory.

"I came back because I need . . . a friend. We *are* friends, aren't we?"

He shook his head, tightened his lips briefly, then replied.

"Friends trust each other. They're honest with each other. Your job won't let you do that. *You* won't let you do that. So, no. We were lovers. Never friends."

Hard to argue that. I didn't try. Instead, I briefly touched my left forefinger to my arm.

"This has bought me time. A few weeks at most. That's how long I have to remember what I saw on the day my parents died."

"I always figured there was something odd—"

He stopped, glared at me as if I'd tricked him into speaking. When it became clear he wasn't going to finish his thought, I said: "Mac has set a trap for a politically influential man. He wants me to be the bait. He *says* the fellow murdered my parents. I'm not sure I believe him. I don't like going blindly into *any* operation, much less one like this. Recalling that day will increase my chances of survival. So I need someone with specialized . . . skills . . . to help me remember. If Mac is telling the truth, I'll return to England, do my job, and serve as bait for his trap."

Alex didn't look sympathetic.

"You didn't answer my question. Why come back here? Why bother me? You're describing an MI-5 operation. You folks are hardly blushing innocents where interrogation is concerned. That's what you're talking about, isn't it? It seems to me that human rights violations are something of a specialty in Northern Ireland."

I was too tired to be provoked. Besides, Alex's opinion of British internal security was less than surprising. Irish-Americans tended to view the IRA as vaguely patriotic, its vi-

olence an understandable response to historical injustices.
Which made *us* the bad guys. I didn't speak my thoughts aloud,
but I did spend a moment thinking about the elderly black man
who'd driven me from the airport. He, too, could lay claim to
historical injustices. Doubtful that Alex would consider *his*
grievances justification for setting off a bomb in downtown
Savannah.

"With the right techniques and access to the right drugs,"
Alex continued, "it wouldn't take one of your cronies more
than a day or two to get the information you're after."

He was right. But the thought of another session like the
one I'd had with Mac encouraged the headache already bloom-
ing behind my eyes. My muscles tensed at the reminder of the
helplessness, the loss of control I'd suffered at his hands. But
the shortcut was worth exploring.

"If I got the drugs and showed you how, would you admin-
ister them?"

Alex lifted his jaw, looked squarely at me.

"No. I'm a cop, not some fucking inquisitor."

I sighed, thinking that there had to be another way to get
what I wanted, one that didn't involve the strain of dealing with
Alex. I considered walking over to the phone, calling a cab, and
catching the next plane out. I could go to some exotic resort.
Rest in the sun. Build up my strength.

But that wouldn't get me answers. And there was no one I
trusted as much as I trusted Alex.

Wearily, I wiped my left hand over my eyes and my clammy
forehead, suddenly aware of how much my arm hurt, of how
grueling the intercontinental flight had been. When I moved
my hand from my face, I was startled to find Alex leaning toward me, hands outstretched, expression concerned.

Our eyes met.

He looked quickly away, straightened, balled his hands into fists. Caring, but trying not to.

Something I understood.

"Why me, Jane?"

I felt like a lawyer presenting closing arguments to a hostile jury.

"You're a skilled interrogator, your instincts are good, and you know me."

He raised an eyebrow.

I responded by sharpening my voice.

"Don't underestimate yourself. You have a talent for getting past my defenses. You always have. When I'm with you, I find myself remem—" I shook my head sharply, dismissing the thought. "You certainly know me well enough to be able to . . . push . . . when I'm least likely to resist. Most important, you're *not* one of my cronies. I can trust you to ask *only* the questions that need to be asked. And I know you won't use the answers to harm me."

Then I made my final appeal, knowing that protecting and caring for people was a reflex for Alex—it didn't matter whether they were friends or relatives, lovers or strangers. That impulse made him a good cop, a good man. It made him easy to manipulate. Easy to betray.

I took a deep breath, reached out, caught the fabric of his sleeve in my hand, allowed headache-induced tears to overflow my eyes and trickle down my cheeks.

"For most of my life, I've run away from that day, terrified. But now, not remembering terrifies me even more. Please, Alex. I need you."

Even as I spoke the last sentence, his expression softened.

I've won, I thought, though I couldn't tell whether I felt more relief or triumph. I didn't allow either feeling to show. I looked at Alex with eyes wide, lips slightly parted, my entire posture emphasizing my defenselessness.

Wordlessly, he stood. He pushed aside the chair that stood between us, encircled me with his arms, and pressed his lips to the top of my head.

I huddled against him.

Safe, I thought. He'll keep me safe.

It was then that I discovered I couldn't stop crying.

16

A strong cup of tea can fix all manner of woes.

Sometimes, a stiff drink works better.

Scotch was my drink of choice. After downing a shot, I felt adventurous enough to risk a bite of cold sausage-and-mushroom pizza.

Some things, even a stiff drink can't fix.

Alex was neatening up the kitchen and turned away from the counter in time to see me drop the soggy slice back into its box.

"I can fix you something *real* to eat."

I shook my head.

"I'm not really hungry." I closed the lid over the pizza. "*That* was a moment of weakness."

He stepped over to the table, scooped up the pizza box, folded it in two, and jammed it into the wastebasket. After detouring briefly to lock the back door, he lingered beside my chair, looking at me, his head tilted and an eyebrow cocked in the direction of my bandages. I recognized the silly half-smile that played across his lips as a prelude to teasing.

He began to say something, then his lips tightened as he thought better of it. He turned away and walked over to the kitchen sink.

"You want another shot? Or some coffee?" he said over his shoulder.

"No, thanks."

He turned on the faucet, squirted dishwashing liquid into the running stream. The dishpan began filling with hot water and suds.

"I'll try to hit the grocery store tomorrow," he said, picking up a stack of plates from beside the sink and immersing them in the dishpan. "I can pick up some fresh produce, maybe some yams. Anything special you want? I've got steaks and chicken in the freezer, and sliced Kentucky ham in the fridge. 'Course, we can always eat out."

Alex's chatter didn't seem to require a response. And the running water made conversation difficult. Which, I suspected, was his intention. I sat staring at his back and asked myself how, exactly, I was going to handle *this*? How, exactly, I was going to regain his trust?

I'd always learned quickly. I offered him more truth.

I waited until he turned off the water, then spoke as if he had just asked about my arm, pitching my voice just loudly enough to be heard over the clatter of the dishes.

"If anyone asks, the official story is that I injured my arm fox hunting on the day after Christmas. That's Boxing Day, which is the highlight, really, of the hunting season. Five minutes into the hunt, my horse was spooked by a grouse breaking cover, and I was thrown. A branch caught me on the way down."

No indication that Alex was listening, but I kept talking anyway.

"The real story involves a kidnapping, a daring rescue, a horrid young bastard with yellow eyes, and a jagged bottle. If you're interested, I'll fill you in on the details."

Alex stopped sloshing around in the soapy water. He pulled a dishtowel from a nearby rack, carefully wiped the water and suds from his hands, dropped the towel onto the counter, and turned. His expression was part surprise, part curiosity, mostly relief.

"I'd like that, Jane."

We sat in the living room, on a sofa that was old, but too comfortable to part with. Reupholstering might have helped, but Alex had solved the problem by covering it with a cream-and-brown afghan and stacking it with wheat-colored pillows. Another, smaller afghan—one his mother had crocheted—was folded over one of the sofa's tall arms.

I told Alex about Winthrup Manor, about Hugh and where his yellow eyes had led me. I told him about the drugs Mac had used, the fire in my flat, and Mac's conversation with Sir William. I kept the narration factual, appealing to the part of him that was strictly cop.

Dusk turned to night. The shadows in the living room deepened, grew solid. The air cooled. We ignored the darkness, shifted in closer, sat with knees touching, eyes locked on each other's face.

". . . so at this moment, Sir William—or someone—is working on a plan to kill me. And Mac is waiting impatiently for his bait to return to the trap."

Alex's reaction was predictably male and reassuring.

"Those fucking SOBs. Don't worry, Jane. We'll work it out."

*   *   *

I was nested into the corner of the sofa, my injured arm supported by a bolster pillow. My shoes were off, my legs pulled up onto the cushions. Comfortable.

I shut my eyes. Just for a moment.

Alex was still beside me, still talking softly, telling me . . . I didn't know what he was telling me. I'd stopped listening to his words. Heard only the comforting rise and fall of his voice.

Tension drained away and left my muscles limp, my limbs too heavy to move. I rested my cheek against the cushioned back of the sofa.

He stopped speaking, and the cushions moved as his weight shifted.

I felt something soft around my shoulders.

Afghan, I thought.

I snuggled into its warmth and slept.

Kitty-mou jumped, crashed through the fiery branches, landed in the center of my robe.

I folded it around her, crawled from beneath the Christmas tree.

The smell of petrol hung in the air.

Thick, oily smoke stung my eyes.

Heat and flames consumed the room.

But I wasn't afraid.

I grasped the bundle to my chest and ran from the Great Hall.

Grandpa was waiting just beyond the heavy doors.

I cried out his name, ran to him.

I wanted him to scoop me up in his arms, to protect me from the fire.

He stood, hands clasped behind his back, staring down at me.

"You let her die."

I shook my head.

"No. I didn't. See? This time, I saved her."

I held out the bundled robe for his inspection, watching his face eagerly.

He bent forward, used thumb and index finger to pull aside the layers of quilted fabric. He frowned.

I lowered my eyes to the center of the bundle.

No Kitty-mou.

I held a raggedly amputated foot. It wore a polished black boot.

I woke up, doubled over and retching violently. Clapped my hand over my mouth as I flung myself from the sofa. I ran across the foyer, into the bathroom that adjoined the guest room. I made it to the toilet just in time. Vomited. Remembered the foot. Alex came into the bathroom, pulled my hair back from my face as I vomited again.

"I'm okay."

I choked out the words, then pressed my lips tight and held my breath, willing myself not to gag again.

He closed the lid on the toilet, then steadied me as I sat down.

I rested my head against the cool porcelain of the tiny washbasin as I groped for the cold water faucet.

Alex's hand was there first. He soaked a hand towel, wrung it out, and gave it to me.

I pressed my face into the cold fabric, blotting my tears, cooling my skin, and soothing my temples. Finally, I lifted my head.

"Sorry," I said.

"Nothing to be sorry about."

He took a paper cup from the dispenser beside the sink, filled it with water, and held it in my direction.

I took the cup, swished the water around in my mouth, and spat into the basin. The bitter, burning taste remained at the back of my throat. I repeated the process, felt better for it.

"Finished?"

I nodded.

Alex brought me a mug of tea loaded with sugar.

I held it briefly, then leaned forward from the sofa and placed the hot mug on the coffee table.

Alex watched, frowning slightly as I rearranged my grip so that I could lift the mug to my lips without spilling the contents. Then he settled back onto the other end of the sofa.

I took a sip and then spent an anxious moment wondering what effect the hot, sweet liquid would have on my stomach. When nothing violent happened, I hazarded another sip, then another.

He waited until I'd polished off half of my tea.

"Bad dream?"

I nodded, knowing my nightmare was likely betrayed by nothing more revealing than rapid eye movement and labored breathing. I didn't talk in my sleep. Individuals with that particular habit rarely completed training—unconscious murmurings were too likely to jeopardize the operative, the mission, the organization.

Alex tipped his head.

"Do you want to tell me about it?"

Tell me about it. That's what I would ask Brian when he awakened with eyes full of remembered horror, crying out "No! Stop!" Please, I would say, tell me about it. Please, let me help you. He never had. He'd never trusted me enough—

I glanced at the clock on the mantel. It was almost midnight. A devil of a time for amateur psychoanalysis, a devil of a time to invite a stranger to tour my subconscious.

Alex was not a stranger.

I'd asked for his help.

"I think the dream was more than imagination," I said.

I described it.

He watched silently as I stared at my lap, using my hands and fingers to define an object that wasn't there.

"The bone is jagged and very white. There are tiny bone fragments where the flesh is . . . torn. But it's not as bloody as you'd expect. Just above the ankle, there are curly black hairs. And there's a knot in one of the laces. Like it was broken, then tied back together. Whoever relaced the boot did it carefully, so the knot wouldn't show."

"Do you know whose boot it is?"

I dug back through the shards of my childhood and found a memory I trusted.

Stavros was beside the limo, down on one knee, tying his shoe. He tugged at the laces, broke one, and cursed.

I thought that he was very funny.

Detachment became more difficult, but I managed it.

"It belonged to Stavros. He was our driver. I suppose it makes sense that the bodies were blown apart. I know the car caught fire and then exploded. I was told that. One of the men who . . . questioned me . . . showed me photos. To help me re- member."

I laughed then. A quick, short release of something that had little to do with humor. And detachment slipped.

I told him about Stavros, about the sidewalk cafes and wash- ing the limo and games of hide-and-seek around the embassy compound.

"I never dared tell my grandfather, or anyone, that I missed Stavros more than I missed my parents. But I did."

Alex reached out, touched my cheek with the back of his fingers, then gently stroked my hair back from my face.

"Why wouldn't you miss him? It doesn't sound like there were any other children around. And it seems as if your parents were very busy people. Stavros was your best friend, wasn't he? Maybe your only friend."

I thought about it, nodded.

"Yes, I suppose he was."

Alex's fingers moved lightly over my right arm from shoulder to wrist. Along the way, he brushed past my breast.

"How bad is it?" he said. "Your arm, I mean?"

It was impossible, really, to feel his fingertips through layers of cotton and gauze. Impossible, but my body responded to the mere suggestion.

My body was not in charge.

I brought my thoughts back to reality by envisioning the mess beneath the bandages. The iodine-stained skin. The caterpillar line of black stitches over an angry red scar. The ragged tears where my activity during the fire had pulled the stitching apart.

"It's healing. Itchy rather than painful. Mostly, it's inconvenient."

Alex's attention was on my lips, but he wasn't listening.

And I wanted nothing more than to be held.

I lifted my right arm carefully, skimmed my fingers down his rough cheek.

"I think it's time I went to bed. Do you want me across the hall or in one of the guest rooms upstairs? And would you mind helping me carry my suitcases in from the verandah?"

I expected irritation, regret, even an argument.

I didn't expect the reaction I got.

"Oh, shit! I wasn't thinking."

Which seemed an overreaction.

Overreaction was followed by haste, which I didn't understand either.

"You stay here. I'll take care of the suitcases."

He walked casually from the room, but his footsteps quickened as he crossed the foyer.

I followed him, watching from the living room door as he deactivated the alarm and switched on the porch light. I crossed the foyer as he peered out through the window adjoining the front door. He paused with his hand on the knob, half-turned, and spoke over his shoulder.

"Damn it, Jane. Listen to me for once. Stay inside."

I didn't understand the situation, but there was no misunderstanding his apprehension. I obeyed promptly, shielding most of my body behind the heavy front door and watching him closely, ready to back him up.

He stepped onto the porch.

The suitcases were there, at the top of the steps, in about the same place as I remembered leaving them. They stood not quite side by side, near ends touching, far ends spread apart, forming a wedge that angled toward the doorway.

Alex approached the suitcases warily, stepped around them slowly, viewing them from all sides.

I'd seen that behavior before, in the members of a bomb squad as they approached a suspicious package left in the Fountain area of Londonderry. I'd watched from a distance, terribly aware of the risk they took. Assembling a bomb was easy. That, I could do. Disarming someone else's work was another thing altogether. Without specialized training, only a fool would attempt it.

Alex was one of the least foolish people I knew. So unless he had skills I was unaware of . . .

He derailed that train of thought.

"Yep, we've definitely got a problem."

Despite his words, the tension was gone from his voice. He turned his back on the suitcases, stepped back into the foyer.

"Hang in there, Jane. I'll be right back."

He went straight through the entry hall, stopped in front of the linen closet that was built into the space beneath the staircase. He opened one of its tall wood doors and took out a pillowcase. As he recrossed the entry hall, he lifted the walking stick from the umbrella stand.

"Do you want to help or just watch?" he said when he rejoined me.

Ego inspires all sorts of stupidity.

I said, "I'll help."

He handed me the pillowcase—cream-colored flannel with burgundy pinstripes—then went back outside.

I followed him, moved beside him when he stopped near the suitcases. In a heap between them was something that might once have been a man's white cotton T-shirt. A rag, I thought. One that was much too large to have been deposited there by the wind.

I took a closer look.

"Fucking hell."

Alex smiled grimly.

"Couldn't have said it better myself."

Not quite hidden beneath the fabric was a curve of sinuous body.

Using the handle of the walking stick like a hook, Alex cautiously lifted the rag away, exposing the snake. Its arrow-shaped head was a rusty orange, its unblinking eyes flat yellow with dark, vertical slits. From the base of its skull to the tip of its tail, the rusty orange color was broken with darker, hourglass-shaped crossbands.

All of my knowledge of snakes came from a single encounter with a rattlesnake in Alex's backyard and one chapter of a colorfully illustrated paperback he'd lent me.

This snake was shaking its tail, but it didn't have a rattle.

I hazarded a guess, based on color.

"Copperhead?"

"Copperhead."

"Poisonous?"

"Oh, yeah."

"Shooting it is out of the question, I suppose."

He laughed.

"The Savannah police are sworn to serve and protect——"

"Snakes?"

"Well, okay, the law's a little vague on that point. But this little guy's hell on rats, which makes him kind of useful."

As he spoke, Alex took the rag from the end of the walking stick and brought it near his face. He took a quick sniff, wrinkled his nose.

"I thought I recognized the shirt. I cleaned the furniture with it last week. Lemon-scented polish. Then I used it to touch up some scratches with wood stain."

He held up the rag for my inspection.

I could see a variety of oily brown blots.

"Dark walnut for the wardrobe in the guest suite and the phone stand in the upstairs hallway. Golden oak for the furniture in our bedroom. The last time I saw this rag, it was in the trash."

He tossed aside the grubby shirt, then moved the walking

stick toward the snake again, approaching it slowly from behind.

"As cold as it is tonight, he should be pretty lethargic."

Alex thrust the handle of the walking stick forward, pressed
it across the snake where its body joined its head, and pinned
the snake against the floor. It writhed violently, its mouth
opened wide.

Definitely not my idea of lethargic.

"Okay, Jane. Open the pillowcase."

I held it with both hands fairly close together, leaving most
of the fabric hanging free.

Alex spared a glance in my direction.

"Good girl."

He bent down, gripped the snake just behind its head, laid
down the walking stick, and picked up the snake. Its belly scales
were dark pink and glossy, and I noticed a large bulge about a
quarter of the way down its body.

Alex noticed, too.

"Snakes like to stay put after they've eaten. Doubtful he
found that meal here on the verandah."

"Someone seems to be sending you a message."

"You might say that."

I thought about Joey's urgent phone call and the conversation I'd overheard in the kitchen.

"This is definitely *not* your imagination."

He looked at me blankly, lifted his chin in the direction of
the pillowcase.

"Get ready."

He guided the snake's body into the bag with his free hand,
then took hold of the edge of the pillowcase.

"You can let go now."

I did as he said, leaving him literally holding the bag. And the snake.

He lowered the copperhead into the pillowcase, angling its snout downward. When it was completely inside, Alex dropped the snake, snatched his hand away, and gave the opening a quick twist shut. The snake seemed content to remain in a motionless lump at the bottom of the pillowcase.

"I'll take our visitor way back into the woods and get your suitcases on my way back in. Take the room across the hall from mine."

Then he offered me the pillowcase.

"Unless you'd prefer to take a late-night stroll?"

Without hesitating, I shook my head.

Alex grinned.

"I didn't think so."

17

Flames shot through the passenger compartment, scorching what was inside. Thick, black smoke boiled up into the sky. The car exploded. Pieces of metal rained around me. Something heavy hit the ground beside me.

I refused to look at it.

Smoke and flames.

Hot. Choking.

Run away. Now! Run away from the thing on the ground. Away from what was left inside the white car. Away from the smoke and flames.

Awake.

I was awake. In Alex's house. Across the hall from the room where he slept. I was safe.

My heart was still pounding with fear reaction as I slipped from the bed. I concentrated on the mundane—and, lately, quite challenging—task of dressing. By the time I pulled on a dark blue sweatshirt, matching sweatpants, and a pair of loafers, my heart rate was back to normal.

Ignoring Alex's open door, I walked down the hall and down the back stairs. I crossed the dark kitchen, slid the switch on the coffeemaker to brew. Alex's system—a cop's response to an unpredictable world.

"I never know when I'll be called away," he'd once told me. "So I always try to have the next pot ready to go. If you're up first, just turn it on."

As I always did when I made the pot, I filled my mug under the running stream before putting the carafe in place. I went out onto the back porch, sat on the top step, and watched the sun rise. I listened to the birds singing, slowly sipped my coffee, and waited for the caffeine to take effect.

I was nearly to the bottom of the mug when I heard the noise of an engine from the other side of the house and recognized it as belonging to Tommy's pickup truck.

Tommy parked and walked around to the back porch. He was in uniform and carrying a white cardboard box labeled Krispy Kreme Donuts. When he saw me, he smiled. Apparently, he had decided how he felt about me.

"G'morning. I'm offering an even exchange. Donuts for coffee. Any takers?"

He tipped the box he held. Through the clear cellophane panel in its lid, I saw at least a dozen donuts.

I returned his smile, then began to rise.

"Alex is still sleeping, but I'm sure he wouldn't want to miss—"

Tommy's casual wave returned me to the step.

"Just sit. I know where the coffeepot is. And if you don't mind, let's let Alex be. It'd be real nice if you and I could sit here and talk awhile."

He tipped his head at the end of the sentence, lifted an eyebrow, made it a question.

I nodded.

Tommy put the box of donuts down on the step, then glanced at my cup and took it from me.

"Black, right?"

"Please."

He opened the screen door and went into the house, leaving the kitchen door standing open. I watched him move around the kitchen with familiar ease, taking a clean mug from the hooks above the counter, pouring the coffee, getting a spoon from the dish drainer, pulling a few feet of paper toweling from the roll beneath the cabinet.

Back on the porch, Tommy sat beside me on the step so that the box of donuts was between us. After handing me my mug and a section of paper towel, he tucked the rest of the toweling beneath a corner of the box. Then he took three hot pink packets of artificial sweetener out of his jacket pocket, tore them open, and stirred the contents into his coffee.

I lifted the lid of the box.

"I couldn't remember what kind you liked," Tommy said, "so I picked up an assortment. After getting a look at you yesterday, I figured you might do well to eat 'em all. It'll take a lot of calories just to get you back up to skinny."

"Where I come from, this is the height of high fashion."

"Starvation being the 'in' look this year?"

"Unfortunately, no one brings me donuts in London."

I selected a chocolate iced donut and briefly held it up for his inspection.

"Does this one look fattening enough?"

"Sure does."

Tommy lifted an iced jelly donut from the box, put the lid

back down. He took a large bite and then a quick smaller bite to keep the raspberry jelly from oozing onto his hand, chewed happily for a moment, then washed the mouthful down with a gulp of diet coffee.

I laughed, which didn't seem to bother Tommy at all.

We sat looking out at the trees, and I waited patiently to find out what was on his mind.

"I wanted to apologize for running out like that last night. Poor thing to do."

"I was so tired, I didn't even notice."

He nodded, sandwiched the word "good" between the final two bites of the jelly donut, and washed everything down with coffee. Then he went back to contemplating the tree line.

"Alex tell you about the weirdness that's been going on?" he said finally.

"No. But I think I experienced it firsthand."

I described the encounter with the copperhead.

"This happened last night?"

I nodded.

"How'd he explain it to you?"

"He didn't."

"I don't suppose he told you about the diamondback he found upstairs in the bathtub, a few days after Christmas? Damned thing was almost six feet long. Or the box of coral snakes left at the front door the next day? Or the cottonmouth that he found on the seat of his squad car day before yesterday?"

"No."

"I didn't think so. 'Course, Lord only knows what he hasn't told *me*. That boy always could keep a secret, and lately . . . I tell you, Jane, I'm real worried. So's Joey. Not that she had *any* details. But she always did know when Alex was in trouble. She asked me for your phone number. Said there was more to you than either Alex or I realized. Smart girl."

He reopened the bakery box with a flip of his finger.

"I think we're dealing with a dangerous stalker," he continued. "I've studied the profiles, seen the stats. People like that only get worse with time. Four incidents—no, damn it, four attacks—in less than two weeks. And those are just the ones I know about for sure. There's one sick puppy after Alex. And I'm afraid that stupid white boy's gonna get himself killed. He won't let me assign people to protect him. Won't even file a fucking report."

He lifted a white-iced donut, bit into it with enough force to rattle any loose fillings, and glowered down at his coffee as he chewed and swallowed. He was undoubtedly frustrated.

Alex often had that effect on Tommy.

On me, too.

"Alex Callaghan is a stubborn ass," I said.

Tommy turned his head, half-surprised by my declaration.

"But I doubt he'll change," I added.

Tommy leaned over, picked up a piece of donut that had fallen onto the step, pitched it in the general direction of the birdbath in the center of the kitchen garden.

"Tell me something I don't know."

"Perhaps I should file a complaint. That last attack was against me, too."

"Yeah! Okay. Good idea."

But apparently it wasn't.

Tommy looked enthusiastic for only a moment, then frowned. He spent another minute attacking the rest of his donut, speaking only after he'd followed up the last crumb with a gulp of coffee.

"Maybe it's best to wait."

"Why?"

"Alex isn't stupid. Or suicidal. There must be something on his mind. Maybe we've got to trust him to call for help when he needs it. That doesn't keep us from watching out for him, though."

Hearing my advice to Joey echoed by Tommy was odd. But the advice was valid, no matter whose mouth it came from. I didn't approve the situation any more than Tommy did, but if Alex was determined to play it solo . . .

"Maybe, just for now, the two of us can watch out for him," I said. "If I were the stalker, I sure as hell wouldn't want to take you on. And we both know that I'm the meanest frigging Brit he's ever likely to encounter."

"Funny. I've been thinking just that. Only in much politer terms, of course."

My laughter was checked by the lack of humor in Tommy's expression.

He put down his donut and coffee, pushed aside the donut box until it was no longer between us, and turned completely in my direction. His dark brown eyes examined my face.

"Look here, Jane. Whatever you do away from Savannah is strictly your business. But I've got a good idea what you're capable of. Have had for months now."

He paused, kept his eyes on mine.

I didn't waste time denying that he knew who I worked for and what I was. Before the Feds had moved in to protect me from an SPD murder investigation, Tommy and Alex had made some informal inquiries and gotten more information than they should have. I doubted the two men would ever realize how thoroughly *they* had been investigated as a result of knowing what they did about me. For Alex and Tommy, privacy was now nothing more than a comforting illusion.

I nodded, acknowledging the worth of Tommy's information.

I didn't change my expression or look away.

He appeared satisfied by my response.

"It seems to me you're one of those people who finds leaving a lot easier than staying," he said. "That thought struck me on Thanksgiving Day. I knew then that it was only a matter of time . . .

"You remember that night. We'd just finished dessert, and I was clearing dishes. Ginnie was changing Zach's diaper, and Tad was in his crib, fussing. Alex went in and got him, brought him back to the living room, and held him like he always does. That's when I spotted you. Watching. Looking kind of, well . . . soft. Then, all of a sudden, something scared you. I could tell. I went to help, but before I could take half a step in your direction, your face went blank. Like a mask dropping into place. Suddenly, I didn't see any expression on your face at all, except maybe a stranger's cool, polite interest.

"I hadn't thought of my daddy for a while, but seeing you . . . *He'd* look at me just that way before he'd take off again. Like he didn't know me. Like he didn't want to know me. For a long time, I thought there was something about me he didn't like. But it was something *in him* kept him from accepting other people's caring. Kept him from caring back. I don't know what happened to make him the way he was, but I think something got broken early on."

He paused for a moment, giving me an opportunity to— what? Contradict him? Tell him I wasn't like his daddy? Explain why I was? Let him know that some people didn't break all at once, that sometimes it took years?

I said nothing.

Tommy sighed, pursed his lips, and nodded his head ever so slightly.

"So I figure, sooner or later, you'll leave again. That's really why I came here at this hour of the morning. I know you're an early riser, and I was hoping to catch you alone. Whether he wants it or not, Alex needs full-time protection. Even with his cooperation, that'd be difficult. But when Joey called you, you came back. So you must still care."

I kept silent. I didn't contradict him. But Tommy was wrong. I'd come back for my own sake, not Alex's. And when I had what I wanted, I would leave again.

Tommy continued speaking.

"You must still care, at least a little. Maybe as much as you can. So I'm asking for your help on this, Jane. I'm asking for your word that you'll stay with Alex until the stalker is history. After that . . ." He shrugged. "I guess after that, whether you stay or go is up to you."

Not much later, Alex came down to the kitchen. Like Tommy, he was in uniform.

Tommy turned, waved casually.

"Hey, slug-a-bed. Grab yourself some coffee and join us. I brought donuts. Been sittin' here, makin' sure Jane doesn't eat 'em all up."

Then he continued the story he'd launched into only moments earlier, in response to the sound of Alex's footsteps on the back staircase.

"So Buchannan— You remember him, don't you, Jane? He's a fat, balding white guy with sergeant's stripes and a beer belly? Well, he tells me they clock this woman doin' forty-five in a thirty and pull her over. The woman's middle-aged, nicely dressed, with sacks of groceries in the backseat of her car. A routine traffic stop. So Buchannan stands back and lets the rookie write the ticket.

"Right away, the woman starts pleading with the kid.

" 'Cain't we talk about this, Officer?' she says. 'Cain't I make a donation or buy a few tickets to the policeman's ball or something?'

"And Buchannan swears the rookie looked right at her and said, clear as can be, 'Ah'm sorry, ma'am. The Savannah police don't have balls.' "

Four donuts later, both men left for the station.

As Tommy walked to his truck, Alex lingered on the porch long enough to drop a kiss on my cheek.

"I need to finish up some paperwork, but I should be done by late afternoon. I'm off tomorrow, and I'll use vacation days after that. That'll give us a block of time to concentrate on your . . . um . . . problem. I have a couple of ideas." He paused. "That is, if that's still what you want."

I nodded.

"It is. Thanks."

"No problem. Hey, don't go wandering, okay? And keep the doors locked." He grinned. "I don't want any snakes getting into the house."

I lingered on the porch a little longer, enjoying 70 degrees and sunshine. Absentmindedly, I scratched at my right arm. Then I looked down at it. It had been ten days, I thought. Or close enough.

I dropped off my mug and the donuts at the kitchen counter on my way upstairs to Alex's bathroom. His medicine cabinet was well stocked, and I found what I needed right away. I cut the dressing from my arm, then used tweezers and a bit of willpower to remove my stitches. One knot at a time, one piece of thread at a time, one quick tug at a time.

Then I washed down the entire area with alcohol.

I was left with several dozen pairs of tiny pink tracks bordering a thin, irregular scar. I made a fist, flexed my arm, and felt the weak muscles quiver.

18

The cashier and the bagger at Winn Dixie were friends.

I could tell. Anyone could.

One was white. One was black. Both were thin. They each wore a short knit skirt, a tight knit top, and lots of rings in lots of places. Fingers, nostrils, lips, ears. Their loose uniform smocks, worn unbuttoned, did nothing to improve their appearances.

It was like shopping in London.

Except these two were not in a hurry.

They examined each item I'd purchased, paused to read the ingredients on a few, asked me about the identity of one of the vegetables, and moved the items ever so slowly from conveyor to bag.

I had time. I was patient. And I only *thought* that they might be stoned. I didn't say it out loud.

Stoned or not, when the explosion outside shattered the plate glass windows and sent cans toppling from the shelves, they were the first to drop to the floor.

They were also among the first to raise their heads.

The bagger stood, turned in a slow, full circle, tugged at one of her earrings.

"Fuck," she said slowly, making it sound religious.

Shoulder to shoulder, she and her friend made their way to the front of the store, stepping over glass, gaping and pointing at the parking lot.

I was behind them. I gaped, too.

The white sedan I'd driven to the market was in flames.

"Whose car *is* that?" the cashier asked.

The bagger shook her head slowly.

"Dunno."

"Mine," I said.

They turned and gaped at me.

The fire department came roaring in, followed by the police.

The fire was extinguished.

A clutter of cops supervised the scene.

One recognized me. A younger cop with a red mustache, thinning red hair, and freckles in between.

"Hey, Jane! Glad to see you back. Your car?"

"Alex's actually. But I drove it and parked it. I was inside the store when it exploded."

He shook his head, turned slowly, looked over the devastation again. Then his green eyes returned to my face.

"Damn," he said.

He thumbed the two-way radio on his shoulder.

"This is Merle—"

Behind him, the sun reflected off the glittering glass that had once been Winn Dixie's display window. My gaze continued upward, drawn to the building's low roof by another glint.

Scope!

"—and we have a—"

I hit the young cop with my left shoulder, knocking him to the ground.

"Gun!" I yelled. And pointed.

The bullet hit the pavement beside us, sent cement chips flying.

Around us, cops flattened themselves on the ground and scrambled to the shelter of the nearest car. They cried out to the civilians to get down, to take cover now! They aimed their weapons at a shooter who was no longer there.

"Tried to kill a cop!" someone muttered. "Torched the car and waited."

Maybe, I thought. Maybe.

As long as selecting *my* car was coincidence.

Reports were filed, headlines made, and glass swept up. The car was towed to the police impound lot. A few hours after that, Alex and I sat down to a dinner of pork chops and peas and mashed potatoes. It was good food for poking at when no one is much interested in eating.

"Does Sir William know you're here?"

I shook my head.

"In theory, no."

"Could someone have followed you? Maybe someone he hired?"

"I was careful, Alex. And a professional assassin would have done a better job, don't you think?"

"Even professionals screw up."

I pondered that possibility as I squashed my potatoes with the back of my fork and watched the gravy run out onto the plate. Then I said: "Perhaps your fellow is escalating."

Alex stiffened, but I ignored his body language and finished my thought.

"He may have recognized your car in the parking lot, assumed you were in the store, and taken the opportunity."

"And mistaken Merle for me? I don't think so."

"Then we're back to coincidence. Which neither of us believes in."

Alex looked down at his plate and rolled his peas around with his fork.

"I'll get some extra cops out here to protect you."

"And your stalker?"

He stabbed a piece of pork chop, then put his fork down on his plate. He lifted his eyes to mine.

"He takes his chances. I can't protect him forever."

"What's going on, Alex?"

"Keep out of it."

He added a curt "please" as an afterthought.

His tone brought to mind poisonous snakes and old colonial flags.

Don't tread on me, I thought. The attitude was typical Alex.

"Okay. Your house. Your rules."

He looked horrified.

"I'm sorry. I didn't mean—"

I brushed the apology aside with a casual sweep of my hand and a twist of my lips.

"I'll try not to interfere, Alex. But what you're doing—the risk you're taking—scares me. And Tommy. And Joey."

"Believe me, I know. But I can't think of any other way to handle it."

"Very well. I suppose all we can do at this point is watch our backs carefully. In the meantime—until one of us decides otherwise——the car was randomly selected. A trap baited for a cop. Any cop. The guy waited, took his shot, and ran away."

He nodded. Lifted his fork again.

"Thanks. Better eat up. Tommy told me to make sure you didn't miss a meal."

After dinner, we baked cookies.

At first, I objected. As Alex pulled mixing bowls, measuring cups and spoons, and cookie sheets from cupboards and drawers, I said: "The identity of a killer is buried in my memory. Someone is delivering reptiles to your doorstep. And there's a sniper after one of us. Perhaps our time could be better spent?"

He paused, regarded me seriously, then shook his head.

"Nope. I can't think of anything better to do, right at the moment."

He moved around the kitchen gathering ingredients and didn't speak again until he was cracking eggs into a large bowl.

"There's nothing threatening about being here in the kitchen with me and making cookies."

He paused, and his statement seemed to require an answer.

"No. There isn't."

"So maybe this'd be a good time to let down your guard. When you concentrate on mixing and measuring, the rest of your mind gets a chance to wander. 'Least, that's been my experience. If you think of something significant, great. If not, we'll have cookies to munch on. Okay?"

I nodded, then took several deep breaths and released them slowly as I made a conscious effort to relax the tension in my jaw, neck, and shoulders.

Alex used a large wooden spatula and began beating together eggs, butter, and brown sugar in a large orange crockery bowl. The bowl clashed terribly with the red tabletop.

"Is your arm strong enough to handle sifting the dry ingredients?"

"I think so."

Following Alex's instructions, I measured and sifted, then added the flour mixture to his bowl.

He stirred some more.

I added vanilla and rum extract.

"My mom used to make these cookies with *her* mother. She told me that one day when I was helping her bake," he said. "So when Joey was little, I made sure she and I made cookies together. Now she has the recipe memorized, too. Someday, when she has kids, she'll probably bake cookies with them."

Alex opened a plastic container, filled a scoop with pecans, and let them slide into the bowl. He repeated the procedure with semi-sweet chocolate chips and again with walnuts.

More stirring.

"The dough's always the same, but the other stuff varies according to what you have in the pantry."

Unexpectedly, I recalled a very different recipe.

The instructor tipped the pipe bomb on end, lifted the battered scoop, and drove it into a barrel of nails. He poured the nails into the pipe. Then he shoved the scoop into a bucket of ball bearings. The third scoop was filled with broken glass.

"The basic components are always the same. But the load varies according to availability and personal preference."

A moment, perhaps two passed before I realized that Alex was standing quietly beside me, waiting. I lifted my eyes to his face and saw sympathy, concern, and something more. I saw a cop's perceptions. An interrogator's perceptions. I tensed, anticipating questions I didn't want to answer.

Alex's lips tightened just a bit.

"Nothing threatening," he said quietly.

He turned away, crossed the kitchen, dug through the refrigerator, and came back to the table with a small cardboard
box. He held it up.

"Raisins?"

I managed an expression of mock horror.

"Ugh! No raisins. Please."

He grinned and tried a little salesmanship.

"They're a marvelous source of nutrition. Lots of iron."

"I still abhor them. Always have. Always will."

Alex sighed mournfully.

"Too bad."

He returned the box to the refrigerator, then detoured to the
silverware drawer and brought several mismatched spoons back
to the table. They were held up for my inspection.

"Choose your weapon."

*"Choose your weapon," Mac said as we stood at the end of the firing
range. I looked at the handguns spread out before me, reached for the one
I'd seen Mac use. He shook his head, grabbed my wrist, lifted my hand,
and put his palm against mine. My hand was slim, my fingers long and
tapered. His hands and fingers were thicker, wider, stronger. "What best
suits me or any other man will not necessarily work for you." He pointed
at the Walther PPK Special. "Try this one."*

I took the smaller spoon and concentrated on dropping
somewhat uniform glops of dough onto the cookie sheets.

The batches moved from raw to baked to cooled to cookie
jar. Alex and I nibbled broken cookies, drank milk, and talked
about nothing in particular. Eventually, the conversation
turned to foods we liked and foods we'd tried. That turned into
a game of one-upsmanship.

Impressing a woman like me was difficult.

Impressing a Marine who'd soldiered in Vietnam was equally
challenging.

There was no reaction on either side to mushy grubs and crunchy bugs. No reaction, except another memory I didn't share with Alex.

There were roaches on the plate, mixed in with the coagulated brown slime that passed as food. The roaches were dead, mostly. Which was a blessing. I dug them out with the tip of my finger and flicked them away, trying not to count. Then I began eating the only food I'd get that day, wondering at what point I'd be hungry enough to eat the bugs, too.

"Endure training," Mac had said, *"and you can endure anything."*

The roaches were the least of it.

Our game moved on to exotic blue plate specials.

"Kangaroo tail soup," I offered.

"Alligator jerky," Alex countered.

"Sheep's eyeballs."

"Monkey brains."

I called for a new game.

"Why now?" Alex asked indignantly. "Are you quitting because I was winning?"

Mac's voice: "Why now, Janie? You buried Brian seven years ago. You didn't quit then, though I thought perhaps you would. Why now?"

"Maybe I felt I owed it to Brian—and to you—to carry on, to serve Her Majesty's government without reservation. I've given as much as anyone should be asked to give. So now I'm asking, Mac. Please, let me go."

I forced a smile and infused it with a little malice.

"Your last few suggestions were making me hungry."

He laughed.

"Okay. Same game. New rules. You have to have tasted it *and* know how to cook it."

He knew I didn't usually cook and foolishly assumed he had an advantage.

I lifted my chin.

"Since you *believe* you were winning, you go first."

"Roast 'possum. You want the recipe from the time you shoot it?"

Suddenly, I was recalling too many faces and too much death.

Suddenly, I was recalling only one face.

Brian lay sprawled at my feet, his eyes staring sightlessly at the ceiling. Beneath him, the scarred plank floor was filthy and littered with scraps of leather. A distraction, however brief, from the wound I didn't want to see. The wound that was in the center of his chest. It was gaping, dark, and terrible. Fatal. I knew that. But I fell to my knees beside him, anyway, and searched for some sign of life. I searched. And I prayed. No miracle occurred.

I tore my mind from the past. Deliberately avoiding Alex's eyes, I pushed a spoon off the table with my elbow and bent over, out of his sight, to retrieve it. As I groped for the spoon, I forced away tears and reestablished emotional control.

I smiled crookedly at Alex as I sat back up.

I ignored his anxious expression.

"Oh, by all means," I said. "Give me the entire recipe."

It took him just a moment to retrieve that line of thought.

"Well, you shoot the 'possum and gut it and hang it in the shed for two days. Unrefrigerated, of course. Then you skin it and cut off the excess fat. After that, you stuff it with seasoned bread crumbs and roast it. Uncovered. For two, two and a half hours. Moderate oven."

There was little surprise in the method of preparation. The rabbit and game birds that my grandfather, Mac, and I had hunted were cooked in much the same manner. Except that, rather than trim off fat, you often had to lard them.

"Sounds tasty."

Alex looked disappointed.

"Haggis," I said.

"I've heard of it. But can *you* cook it?"

"The servants used to make it for my grandfather as a special treat. I'd sit on a stool beside the stove and watch them."

I closed my eyes, ticked off the steps on my fingers as I recalled the recipe.

"You take a sheep's heart and liver. Mince it up with suet, onions, and oatmeal. Season it well. Stuff it into the sheep's stomach. Then boil it into a nice pudding."

I opened my eyes in time to see Alex wrinkle his nose.

"Gross!"

"I win, don't I?"

"Not yet, you don't."

His eyes narrowed as he stared across the kitchen at the ragged row of cookbooks on a shelf above the cellar door. Unlike the couple of cookbooks on top of the refrigerator, these were old and dusty, promising more arcane recipes.

Alex looked at me and smiled. Wickedly.

I held my breath.

"Beef tongue—"

I exhaled, shrugged. If that was the best he could do . . .

"—smothered in a thick, sweet raisin sauce."

I shuddered and threw a pot holder at him.

We sat together on the sofa in the living room, caught the end of an *X-Files* rerun, then watched the late news.

Alex looked good on TV. Sincere. Credible. Handsome. He stood with the devastated store behind him, spoke of the investigation in progress and said they had several strong leads. Of course, the Savannah Police always encouraged the public to call them if they saw anything suspicious.

The man on the sofa beside me muttered, "Fucking politician."

After that, we watched the sports report, then the weather. A pleasant looking fellow in a conservative suit and tie talked about high pressure systems, a day or two without rain, and temperatures in the sixties.

Alex sighed.

"Nice. But boring." He suddenly laughed. "Actually, it hasn't ever been as much fun since Captain Sandy went off the air."

I noted the expression on Alex's face and knew I was being set up again.

"Who is Captain Sandy?" I asked cautiously.

"The local weatherman. Years ago. Back before the news was in color. In those days, of course, there was no Doppler weather radar or spiffy animated weather maps. Captain Sandy had a boring wall map with weather symbols that looked like they were cut out of cardboard. He used a wooden pointer to show you where things were. But I watched him anyway, because he was a sailor, and he always dressed according to what the weather was going to be. Every night, just as he came on, they'd play his special song. Give me a minute. I bet I can remember the words."

He began whistling a very tentative hornpipe.

"Got it!" he said, half a dozen bars later. "Now you have to imagine I have a raincoat and gum rubber boots on. And I'm dancing, okay?"

"Right-o. I'm picturing you wearing green Wellies with your bright yellow slicker and doing a jig."

"Oh-oh, what's the weather going to be?

"Here's a man who knows, so let's take a look and see.

"Here is Captain Sandy with the weather he has found,

"For Savannah and for Charleston and the counties all around."

✢   ✢   ✢

I laughed until my sides hurt and tears ran down my cheeks. Laughed as Alex put his arm around my shoulders and pulled me close. Then laughter died, replaced by longing.

I wanted him.

I had never stopped wanting him.

He gently shifted me onto his lap and wrapped his arms around me, surrounding with his warmth, his strength.

I settled in willingly, tipped my chin upward as he brushed his lips along the curve of my neck, around my ear, across my cheek. Then his hands followed the trail of his lips, and he cupped my jaw and cheeks in his palms.

The soft, warm caresses continued, soothing tension and encouraging desire. His lips lingered on my eyelids, skimmed the bridge of my nose, played at the corners of my mouth.

Then he kissed me. He held my face trapped between his hands, pressed his lips against mine, and demanded response.

I rested my left palm against his chest, surrendered intellect, embraced instinct . . .

A mistake. I was making a mistake.

Beneath my hand, his throbbing heart summoned memories of the day he'd been shot. He would die, too. Just like everyone else. Just like Brian. How could I have forgotten?

I panicked, suddenly wanting nothing more than to push him away, push memory away, flee the house, run.

Where?

I couldn't trust the man I worked for.

I needed access to my past.

There was nowhere but here.

Desire turned cold-blooded.

Alex was a man like any other. I needed him. I would use him.

I slid my hand downward until my palm rested against his belt buckle, hooked my fingers beneath it, promising pleasure.

It had worked on other men. Bought me information, contacts, protection.

No response from Alex.

He took a deep, shaky breath.

"Are you sure, Jane? Is this what you really want?"

Tension tightened his voice.

Urgency shaped the lines of his body.

But he would retreat from passion to friendship. If I asked him to.

He would never use me.

I could trust him.

The reminder rekindled longing.

Lingering fear inspired urgency.

I let go of his buckle, moved my hand to the back of his neck, pushed my fingers through his hair, pulled him to me. I opened my mouth to his, accepting—no, seeking—a single moment of exquisite, mindless pleasure.

19

I dreamt I was back in Australia.

The radio was tuned to a Melbourne station. Harp music—a traditional Gaelic tune, light and airy—poured from the tiny speaker. Across the room, loud male voices argued yesterday's football game.

Ignoring the distraction, I bent closer to the table, encouraging twin wings of dark hair to sweep forward and shield my face. I focused on the music as my fingers performed another task altogether.

One voice cut across the others, breaking my concentration.

"I bet the sheila knows."

"Hey, Morgana," another man called out, "just before he scored for New-bloody-Castle, wasn't it O'Malley that elbowed Simpson in the nose?"

I kept my eyes on the device I was building, paused with tweezers midair, one end of a wire waiting to be anchored to the timer. I took a breath, answered in an accent as broad as theirs, answered knowing that I had a reputation for being as unstable as the explosives I handled.

"It was that sod O'Brian. And if I don't get some quiet, it'll be us, not the Sydney Opera House, that blows up tonight. Either way, the explosion'll be a real ripper."

I lifted my head, swung my hair back, let them glimpse a lunatic grin, then hunched over my work again.

For the next hour, only harp music filled the small room.

I drifted up from sleep, smiling at the single moment of humor in that hellish assignment. I opened my eyes, found Alex awake, head on his pillow, looking at me.

"Pleasant dream?"

"Uh-huh."

"About what?"

"Building a bomb."

He rolled over, swung his legs off the side of the bed, sat up. Reached back across the bed and ruffled my hair.

"Just an old-fashioned girl," he said.

I sat up against the pillows in the warm bed and listened to the sounds coming from the bathroom. The shower was running, the waterproof radio hanging in the stall was tuned to a local station, and Alex was singing. The weather report—river flood warnings in effect for the Savannah River at Burtons Ferry, the Ogeechee River at Eden, and the Ohoopee River at Reidsville—had been followed by a song about a lost love. Alex joined in on the chorus.

"That's my girl, my whole world, but that ain't my truck."

Then a cheerful female voice announced it was time for one from Garth. This seemed to please Alex, who belted out the lyrics to the energetic song with considerable enthusiasm. His voice was pleasant, the words clear, and the song's rhythm an upbeat accompaniment to the exercises I was doing.

Work on flexibility first and then build strength, Dr. Bowers had said when she'd given me the exercises. Discomfort was acceptable. Pain was not. Deciding where the line lay between the two was up to me. And she hoped to God I'd exercise common sense.

"He says it's really kinda simple, keep your mind in the middle . . ."

I listened to Alex and Garth as I methodically rotated my shoulders, loosening muscles. Slowly, carefully, I stretched my biceps by extending my arms straight out in front of me. Palms down, palms up, then a gentle compression achieved by bending both arms at the elbow and pressing my palms together. I extended my arms out to the sides—palms up and down and meeting above my head—and then I was ready to repeat the entire sequence again. And again. That left the muscles in my right arm quivering and the song at an end. I pushed myself to do another two repetitions. The activity encouraged the repetitive buzz of the song's chorus through my mind.

"He's got a fever, fever, fever, fever . . ."

Poor thing. Perhaps a few aspirin . . .

The water turned off, and Alex stepped out of the shower. Which was a nice distraction from the tight band of discomfort across my upper right arm. He worked at staying fit, and it showed.

He noticed me watching him, did a bouncy little jig for

my benefit, then wrapped a towel around his waist. He stepped over to the sink, spread a layer of shaving cream on his face, began scraping at his beard with a safety razor. Paused.

"I have to go back to the station," he said, his eyes on the mirror. "I need to do the paperwork that I didn't finish yesterday and see what's happening with the shooting."

He went back to shaving.

I bent my knees, folded my arms across them, hoping the change in posture would relieve my aching muscles. It didn't. I considered having some aspirin myself, perhaps as a prelude to breakfast, then told myself to get a grip and think about something else.

"While you're out, I'm going to work on my next book," I said. "The manuscript is due in August, and I've got to re-create the material I lost in the fire. By the way, I bought a laptop."

Actually, if you counted the one that was now nothing more than charred components, I'd bought two.

" 'Bout time."

During his convalescence, Alex had embraced computer technology with fanatic fervor, eventually condemning my portable electric typewriter as heretical. Never mind that I liked it.

The icon of his new faith was visible from the bed, on the opposite end of the bedroom suite, within easy reach of his massive rolltop desk. The PC sat rather disconcertingly atop a solid, centuries-old George II kneehole writing table.

My conversion had been prompted by a repairman judging my typewriter beyond resurrection.

"Mac or PC?" Alex asked.

"One of the new Macs."

"Nice."

High praise indeed.

Alex poured himself a cup of coffee, loaded it with sugar and half-and-half, then settled down across from me at the kitchen table.

I pushed a plate of toast toward him, then reached for the smaller of the two jars that shared the center of the table with the salt and pepper shakers. I twisted the yellow lid off the kettle-shaped jar of Marmite, dipped out a bit of the savory spread on the tip of my knife, and spread a thin, dark brown layer on my toast.

As he always did, Alex wrinkled his nose at the Marmite's yeasty smell and reached for the one-pint Mason jar half-filled with peach preserves. He dolloped preserves into the center of a piece of toast, then folded it over to create a drippy triangle.

I waited until he'd had a bite and washed it down with coffee, then ventured back into dangerous territory.

"That copperhead the other night might have killed you. Why *not* make an official report?"

He shook his head.

"It would have hurt like hell, but the bite isn't lethal."

"In my book, that still makes it intent to commit GBH."

Alex paused mid-bite, raised an eyebrow.

"Grievous bodily harm, which is similar to assault with a deadly weapon. And I gather this isn't the first attempt. Coral snakes *are* lethal."

Alex chewed the bite of toast carefully, swallowed. He wiped the edges of his mouth with a napkin, lifted his chin, and stared straight at me.

"As I told Tommy, those previous incidents were strictly my

imagination. Nothing happened that was worth filing paperwork on."

Unless he was killed. Then, I suspected, he expected his unofficial "imaginings" to be used as the basis for a formal investigation. No wonder Tommy had been angry.

I wasn't too happy, either.

I met Alex's eyes, let a little annoyance show.

"Am I imagining things, too?"

He didn't answer.

I used a bit of toast to mop up an invisible dab of Marmite from my plate, considering how I wanted to react. Beyond, of course, keeping my eyes open and avoiding having some figment of Alex's imagination crawl up and bite me. I popped the piece of toast into my mouth, picked up my coffee mug, and found it nearly empty.

"Buggers," I muttered.

I took my mug and Alex's over to the coffeemaker and filled them from the carafe. All the while, I thought about willful, duty-bound men. They seemed to be my particular curse.

Brian was dead now.

A reminder *not* to care too deeply about Alex.

I could live with him. I could sleep with him. I could use him. And then I could walk away.

Of course I could.

"Where'd you learn to handle snakes like that?" I said when I'd returned to the table with our coffee.

Alex seemed relieved by the change in topic.

"From a buddy of mine, used to live down the road. We met one summer, when we were fishing along the river. Well, actually, he'd just come down to the river. I was stuck out on a tree branch overhanging the river. I'd crawled out on it to retrieve my lure, couldn't figure out how to get back down. Willie rescued me. And *didn't* laugh. I was twelve. He was maybe fifteen, probably been living on his own for a couple of years. He never went to school as far as I could tell. Could barely read. But the things he knew . . .

"He treated me like, well, more like a son than a brother. Seemed surprised at how ignorant *I* was. He said he always figured that white boys were smart, and I'd gone and proven him mighty wrong. He taught me to handle snakes and snare small game, showed me how to catch cooters—turtles—and cook 'em up into a passable soup."

Alex reached out, lingeringly slid two fingers over the Mason jar, touch rekindling memory.

"I bought these at the farmer's market in Garden City. The fire chief's daughter-in-law makes them, and they're real good. But I don't think I'll ever find peach preserves that tasted quite as good as Willie's. He'd make them over a wood fire. Out back, behind the two-room house he lived in. His daddy left him the house—wasn't much more than a shack, really—and a hundred acres of marshland along the Ogeechee. Half of those acres are high and dry. As close as they are to Savannah, they're worth a fortune to a developer nowadays."

"Is that the same Willie who owned the bait shop?" I didn't give Alex time to look surprised. "I noticed the shop on the way from the airport. The cabby told me about him."

"Yeah, the same Willie, the same house. Taxi driver tell you he drowned?"

I nodded.

"He pointed out the very bridge."

Alex sighed.

"You heard about the ghost."

"Oh, yes. The story makes a nice addition to my collection of local lore."

I'd heard my first Southern ghost story before I'd arrived in Savannah. As she gave me directions to Savannah, the young woman at the car rental in Atlanta told me I would be traveling along some of the state's oldest roads. For generations, slaves and, later, chain gangs had toiled to build the roads through the swamps. Fever, exhaustion, and physical abuse had claimed many victims. Some locals believed that those so cruelly treated in life walked unhappily even in death.

Since then, I'd heard other stories, some of them from Alex. But he'd never mentioned Willie. I soon found out why.

"Well, Willie isn't folklore, and that story is crap."

He said it belligerently, as if he'd said it before and then ended up defending his words.

"Most of those stories are," I said mildly.

His chin went down, the tight line of his lips relaxed, and he nodded.

"Willie was my friend. You've probably seen his picture. It's in the bedroom, on the wall behind my desk. Willie and me with our fishing gear and a string of fish, showing off for the camera. I think I was just out of high school. My mom took it, developed and printed it herself."

I remembered the black-and-white photograph. In it, two young men looked straight at the camera, chins lifted, expressions open and innocent. Except for the differences in race, the men were very similar in appearance—tall and lanky, angular in a way that promises beauty in the adult male. Sunlight sifted through the trees, framing them with shafts of light and shadow. The foreground was dark. Behind them, the river sparkled. The photo was idyllic, yet expectant. Like the promise of a thunderstorm on a hot summer day.

"That photograph is art," I said. "Your mom had a real talent."

"Yeah, she was a remarkable lady."

He smiled sadly, took a quick breath, continued.

"Anyhow, Willie always talked about opening a bait shop and making his fortune selling worms and shiners. He started the business on his front porch, just before I left for 'Nam. Actually did well enough that he had electricity *and* indoor plumbing by the time I got home. It was a sad day when I found him floating under that bridge. River was real low that year, or he might have been washed right out to sea. As it was . . ."

He shook his head, dismissing the memory.

"Turned out that my mom's picture was the only one ever been taken of him. The newspaper cut it down to a head-and-shoulders shot for his obituary."

Alex left for work.

I spent the afternoon writing.

I moved into the library at the front of the house, turned on the gas fireplace to take the chill from the room, set my laptop on the oak table, turned on the brass desk lamp, and settled into one of the comfortable leather chairs. I stared at the glowing screen, cursing the electronic page for being as difficult to fill as its fiber-based template.

Sometimes I hated writing.

Most often, it was merely difficult. Pulling words into sentences and building sentences into coherent paragraphs was like walking through the thick, sweet sorghum Alex poured over his corn cakes. Progress was made through habit and persistence.

Motivation came from without—my publisher's deadlines, my agent's suggestions, my readers' expectations.

At other times, the words flowed onto the page, my writing an impulse driven by need. I understood that need. My writing enabled me to excise wounds, exorcise demons, impose order on chaos. The best of Andrew Jax's world was created from the worst of mine, and the resulting scenes were the ones that readers related to, that reviewers pointed to. Book after book, the reviews repeated the same descriptions. "Emotional." "Bloody and brutal." "Raw." "The kind of story you'd expect from Murdock." Whether the commentary was a blessing or a curse depended on the reviewer.

I typed a sentence. Highlighted and deleted it. Typed another sentence, did the same. I spent half an hour accomplishing nothing, then decided to blame lack of inspiration on hunger. It was as good an excuse as any.

I went to the kitchen, fixed myself a tuna salad sandwich, and stood at the back door as I ate it. My gaze wandered along the flagstone path, following it across the fenced garden, beneath a rose arbor, and through a dog-eared gate. The path wound through flowerless clusters of magnolias, oleanders, and dogwoods, eventually ending at the treeline. There, a clearing between two massive oaks marked the beginning of a trail that led down to the Ogeechee River and the sturdy dock that Alex and his father had built.

Alex loved that patch of swampy forest. When we walked there together, he would often tell me of his childhood, of shrieking along the paths with a mob of children as they pretended to be guerrilla forces escaping into the sanctuary of their swamp. Alex had grinned sheepishly, confessed that he and Tommy had often bloodied each other's noses fighting for the privilege of being Francis Marion, aka the Swamp Fox. The

Robin Hood-style hero—whom I'd never read of in *our* history
books—led a band of American revolutionaries against the vil-
lainous British Redcoats.

Despite my dismay that my ancestors were cast as the bad
guys, I'd enjoyed Alex's stories. But his childhood playground
frightened me, as had the dark forest behind my grandfather's
house.

The first time I'd peered down the gloomy path to the
Ogeechee River and felt only terror, I'd convinced myself that
a recent assignment in Belfast—no less nightmarish than
childish imagination—had compounded an atavistic fear.
Nearly dying in Alex's woods had simply reinforced that fear.
In the months before I'd left Savannah, I'd attempted, with
limited success, to pacify unreason by frequently walking
alone through the swampy woodland. Now I suspected that
my fear had its roots in Greece, beneath a forest of twisted
olive branches.

I stared out at the tree line behind Alex's house, studying the
ragged horizon created by the tall oaks and pines and the scrub
between them. Then I brought my focus forward, to the
shorter, wider magnolias spotting the swatch of yard beyond
the house. If I looked at a particular grove off to the left, I
could almost imagine that they'd been planted in rows. Long
cultivated rows with the sun dappling the earth between them.

Row after row of olive trees. Short and twisted.

Dizzily, abruptly, I found myself beneath them.

Running.
Running away as fast as I could.
He'd shoved my face against the glass, forced me to
see—

Something horrible. Something I didn't want to remember.

Then he'd swung me around, slammed me back against the car, pinned me there with his hand around my throat.

I couldn't breathe.

Couldn't move.

I stared up into eyes that were yellow, flat, deadly. Like the copperhead's.

"Talk about this and you'll end up like them."

Then he let me go.

I ran.

Ran until I stumbled and fell.

I scrambled forward on all fours, scraped my bare legs against the rocky soil, hid behind the nearest tree. I huddled there, fist against my mouth, listening, not making a sound.

Birds sang in the distance. A gentle wind rustled the leaves overhead. Sunlight danced on the dry earth.

"Yellow eyes," I murmured.

Had I actually *remembered* seeing those eyes or simply assigned them to the face of my nightmare?

Memory or imagination?

I couldn't tell.

But I was angry anyway. Furious.

I wrenched my eyes away from the trees, sought focus for my unspent rage. At the extreme corner of the grounds, a long six-foot-tall mound of dirt and stacked bales of hay created an ideal shooting range. I'd often practiced there.

As I looked at it, I could almost feel the Walther in my hand.

My hand flexed as I imagined myself taking careful aim at a man with yellow eyes.

I would pull the trigger.

Again and again and again.

I would kill him.

Again and again and again.

Enough!

I took a deep breath, curbed runaway emotions with a dose of logic.

I had no weapon. No Walther. Not even my tiny Beretta.

My hand and arm relaxed, the muscles along my shoulder and spine followed.

I began thinking about a weapon, not a target.

It was easy enough to buy something locally. There were people in Georgia even Alex didn't know of. Perhaps I should make a few phone calls, and, after that, take a drive—

I shook my head again, recognizing the impulse for what it was.

Anxiety. The need to run away, to escape. Now.

A bad impulse.

I would follow my plan.

I would control my emotions.

I would sit down and write.

I forced myself to finish my sandwich, poured myself some orange juice instead of more coffee, then took the large glass back with me to the library. I returned to my chair, returned my fingers to the keyboard and my eyes to the blank screen.

I spent a few minutes stretching my right arm, took a bathroom break, downed a couple of aspirins, and returned to the computer. I found a thought and spun it into a scene.

"Screwing is one thing. Marriage is another altogether."
Jax sat with his chair tipped back, feet on the windowsill. The trio
of pigeons just beyond the soles of his wing-tip shoes focused their

beady eyes on him and cooed encouragingly. He often shared his donuts with them, so they always listened patiently.

That their loyalty was so easily bought put the pigeons on Jax's short list of valued confidants. They shared the list with Fast-Hands Eddie, who was a deaf-mute and a damned good pickpocket, and Jamie McMurphy, who had grown up with Jax at St. Vincent's Home for Boys. In spite of the good Sisters' best efforts, Jamie had not gone on to become a priest. He was the best second-story man on Chicago's North Shore.

As Jax tossed the last piece of a raspberry-filled jelly donut into the pigeons' midst, it occurred to him that his short list now included Millicent.

"A mistake," he told the pigeons.

That mistake, he was sure, had led to the shocking thought he'd had earlier that morning. He'd been lying with his lean body curved around Millie's softer, rounder form and his left hand tucked into the warm nook between her breasts. The thought of marriage had crept, unannounced, into the midst of the slightly smug contentment he always felt after they'd made love.

"Fucking impossible!"

His vehemence startled the pigeons into a brief retreat.

"What's impossible?"

Jax put his feet on the floor, swung around on the chair's squeaky metal casters, looked beyond the battered grey metal desk and a pair of threadbare orange client chairs, across the stretch of cracked green linoleum. Millicent stood in the doorway that connected his office to the reception area. He'd been so preoccupied that he hadn't heard her come in.

Dangerous if it'd been Marty Morris instead of her, he thought. Then I'd have been too dead to worry about marriage.

That snapped his thoughts back to Millicent.

She wore a sky-colored dress that clung to her body and matched

*her eyes. Her blonde hair, which had slipped like raw silk through his
fingers the night before, was pulled back in a neat French twist. She
smelled faintly of lilacs.*

*Jax couldn't help himself. He imagined her naked. Which re-
minded him of how he'd left her that morning. Which made him
think of marriage. Which made him angry all over again.*

*She crossed the room, graceful and completely innocent despite her
walk and the three-inch-tall fuck-me heels she wore. She dropped the
morning mail in the wire In basket at the corner of his desk, leaned
forward, and landed a kiss on Jax's forehead.*

"What's impossible?" she repeated.

*For a moment, he couldn't remember. He shook his head, peeled
his eyes from an up-close-and-personal view of her cleavage, and
struggled to recapture his anger.*

"Marriage."

He said it aggressively, wanting an excuse to argue with her.

She flashed him a bright smile.

"You're right. Now about the Winslow case . . ."

The words seemed to flow from nowhere, one thought leading
smoothly to the next. Like beads onto a waxed string. I finished
the scene, but the mood remained. The odd detachment. The
ability to convert thought into words with no conscious filter
in between.

I exploited it.

I began typing a story that was not about Andrew Jax or his
girlfriend, Millicent. It had no action sequences in the usual
third-person. There was nothing in the writing that my alter
ego, Max Murdock, would ever claim.

It was not a work of fiction.

I wrote from a child's perspective.

I wrote as Jane Nichols.

I wrote what I feared.

And what I absolutely remembered.

It was to have been a holiday—an unexpected treat.

Why not let her come to Delphi with us? my mother had said. As it is, we spend too little time together.

My father had agreed.

I sat beside our driver, Stavros. He was my friend, always teaching me things like how to wax a car properly and how to say important things in Greek. My parents talked quietly together in the backseat.

From a side road, a battered black Mercedes pulled out in front of us.

Stavros tapped the brakes, avoiding a collision.

The old car accelerated away, belching dark smoke from its exhaust. But the steep, narrow road was too much for it. The old car slowed.

Within moments, only a car's length separated us from the Mercedes' rusty bumper. There was no room to pass unless the Mercedes pulled over.

Stavros cursed loudly, laid on the horn.

I listened carefully, memorizing these new Greek words.

The Mercedes drifted toward the right shoulder.

Stavros accelerated, nosing our car forward.

The Mercedes abruptly changed direction, rammed us, and sent our car careening across the road.

The silver crucifix that dangled from the rearview mirror danced at the end of its chain, glinting in the sun.

Stavros hauled on the steering wheel. The car skidded out of control anyway. It crashed through the twisted branches of the olive trees bordering the road and stalled.

I was thrown from the seat, slammed against the dashboard, and landed in a heap on the floor. My face was just inches from Stavros's polished black boots. His right foot moved frantically as he tried to restart the car.

Behind me, the door opened.

I had forgotten to lock it.

I glanced over my shoulder.

A man leaned into the car. A stocking mask hid his face. He held a gun, aimed it past me, fired. Something warm and sticky hit my cheek and neck, my shoulders and arms.

The man pointed the gun into the backseat.

My father shouted, "No, not my—"

The man fired twice. His second shot silenced my mother's screams.

I tried to get away, tried to claw my way past Stavros's unmoving legs.

The man grabbed the back of my dress, dragged me from the car, dropped me to the ground.

I stared upward, into the gun's barrel.

"Sorry, love," he said. "You weren't supposed to be here."

At three o'clock, I saved the document, called it simply "Jane." Then I closed it. Fewer than five hundred words, and I was exhausted.

I didn't reread it. Couldn't.

I tucked the electronic arrow down into the lower left-hand corner of the screen, cueing the screen saver to come on. It was an animated Cheshire cat that I'd found somehow appealing when I'd seen it demonstrated at the electronics store. The cat faded, one body part at a time, until it was merely a smile, then gradually reappeared. Though I hadn't tinkered much with the speed with which the cat vanished and reappeared, I'd made one modification to the screen saver. I'd turned off the babbling, manic laughter that accompanied the cat's antics.

I stood, rolled my shoulders, and walked away from the computer.

20

The fog rolled in after sunset.

Alex was out in it.

He'd called on his cellular phone, apologized for being late, and then described an upscale neighborhood on the eastern city limits bounded by Gwinnett, Bonaventure, and Pennsylvania.

"I'm on my way to a whorehouse."

"So glad you told me. Remember, use a condom."

For a moment, nothing but the wash of static carried over the line. Then there was a quick snort of laughter.

"Wouldn't have known about the place, except one of the johns had a conscience. Called 911 from a pay phone. Seems he walked into the house on Kentucky Avenue and noticed several of the girls were just kids. So he walked out again. Dispatch said the guy was really upset, kept sayin' he'd just gotten into town and all he was after was some good, clean fun. What the hell did he expect?"

I mimicked his accent.

"Ah know what you mean. Damn tourists! Should have 'em all shot at the Chatham County line."

He laughed, which had been my intent.

"Gotta go," he said. "I'll be home as soon as I can. And I'll bring dinner with me."

By seven o'clock, the fog was so thick that I couldn't see beyond the house. It reminded me of the fogs that sometimes enveloped London—swirling, vaguely romantic, tremendously appealing. I decided to enjoy it from the front steps.

Actually, I used the fog as an excuse to have the cigarette I'd denied myself all day long.

The closet in the library was deep and narrow, lined with pegs, and cluttered with shoes, outerwear, and odd pieces of sports equipment. Just inside the door, a dark green, oilskin drover's coat hung between a pair of dusty golf shoes and a light blue nylon windbreaker.

I took the drover's coat from the hook, slipped into it. I'd seen Alex wear the coat when he fixed the car or did yard work during inclement weather. It was patched in several places, and its lower sleeves were smudged with grease. Comfortably large on Alex, the coat was huge on me.

I did up the buttons, briefly turned my head into the corduroy collar, caught a whiff of the fabric. It smelled, lightly and not unpleasantly, of wood smoke and fish—a smell that seemed almost part of the fibers and suggested camping trips long past.

For some reason—and certainly not because of the smell—the coat reminded me of the tweedy woolen jacket my grandfather wore when he worked in his rose garden. I shoved my pack of cigarettes and a lighter into one of the coat's deep pockets, turned off the alarm, slipped out the front door, and pulled it shut behind me.

I stood for a moment in the shadow of the verandah, letting my eyes adjust to the darkness. Satisfied that I was alone, I sat on the top step with my back against one of the house's massive columns. Moisture condensed on my face, a pleasant contrast to the warm, dry cocoon the coat created.

My light flared briefly in the darkness, reflecting eerily off wisps of fog. I lit my cigarette, inhaled a lungful of nicotine, felt my muscles relax as I exhaled. After that, I smoked slowly, savoring the treat, pleased that I'd resisted the temptation to break my resolution of months earlier and smoke in the house.

Old, bad habits would be too easy to slip back into. Earlier novels had been written with a full coffee cup and an overflowing ashtray beside my typewriter. I'd given up my typewriter and my cigarettes. Next, I was sure, I would be convinced to drink decaffeinated coffee. One step beyond that, and writing would be impossible. Perhaps I'd take up piano.

Near the end of my cigarette, I stood and walked down the steps. Beside the steps were flower beds bordered by stacked flagstones. In the warmer weather, the beds overflowed with bright perennials—bleeding hearts, foxglove, coral bells, and bellflowers—in shades of white, pink, and lavender.

I bent briefly, snubbed my cigarette in the damp mulch between some spiky clumps of ornamental grass. Then, almost without thinking, I field stripped it—crushed the butt between thumb and forefinger, tearing the paper. I scattered the shreds of tobacco, rolled the paper into a tiny wad, then tucked it and the filter into my pocket.

I'd acquired my smoking habit not in front of a typewriter, but during the long weeks of a fruitless stakeout. As the match had flared in the shelter of her hands, the operative from whom I'd bummed my first fag offered a warning along with a light.

"Nothing," she said, "clues a suspect onto us faster than an accumulation of cigarette butts."

Her name was Josephine Jones—JoJo—and, during my first few years with the organization, we were often assigned together. She was systematic and logical, rarely intuitive. A leveling influence, Mac had called her. We were on assignment at Ballyshannon when her car blew up with her in it.

I took a deep breath, considered having another cigarette, then froze as I heard a footstep crunch on the driveway's crushed pecan shell surface. I focused in the direction of the sound and saw nothing but swirling fog.

Noiselessly, I stepped back into the flower bed, crouched beside the steps in the deep shadows at the front of the house.

Now the footsteps approaching the house were more cautious, making only the slightest noise with each new step. Visibility was no more than five feet, so I doubted I'd been seen. But I knew the smell of my cigarette would linger in the damp night air.

Long past time I gave up smoking.

A figure wearing a hat, dark jeans, and a waterproof poncho emerged from the fog. A canvas sack hung from one of his shoulders. He wore leather gloves. Undoubtedly, a Browning 9mm was somewhere near at hand.

It was foolhardy to startle an armed man.

I cleared my throat noisily, stood slowly, held my hands wide spread and away from my body. I waited, giving him a moment to register my identity. Then I leaned back against the white balustrade, dug the pack of cigarettes from my pocket, shook one out, and lit it.

"Damn it all, John! You scared the hell out of me."

＊   ＊   ＊

We sat, side by side, on the bottom step, alert for the sounds of an approaching vehicle.

"Polite people call before dropping by. It keeps them from getting shot. Which I would have done, if I'd had a gun."

John grimaced.

"Sorry, but I wasn't planning a visit."

"Worse yet. Means you were skulking about and got caught. Sad, what old age does to a man. Happy birthday, by the way. Fifty-four, isn't it?"

"Fifty-three, thank you very much. And I wasn't skulking. I was checking the bloody perimeter."

"On whose orders?"

"Mac said something about protecting you."

I tensed. Mac had betrayed me after all, I thought. He was endangering Alex just as he had the other residents of my building in London. If anything happened to Alex because of him ... After I'd killed Sir William, Mac would be safe nowhere.

I took a long drag on my cigarette, exhaled slowly, and, when I could do it without emotion, spoke.

"Is there some reason I need protection?"

"That's something only you know. The arson team reported that the fire started inside your flat. In the bedroom closet."

I pressed my eyes shut briefly, shook my head, cursing myself for assuming Mac's people were the only ones who had entered my flat.

"Bad news?" John said.

"Joey—Alex's sister—called me. She left a message on my answering machine and included her phone number. With an area code. And someone took a shot at me yesterday."

John accepted the information as matter-of-factly as I offered it.

"Mac was right to send me."

I sighed.

"Yes, he was. When did you arrive?"

"This morning. I bought a motorbike without a title for cash. An older Harley. It's quite nice. I rode out here and set up shop in a shack not too far away, in the nearest habitable structure along this stretch of bug-infested swamp."

"An abandoned bait shop?"

"Yes, as a matter of fact."

"Talk is, Willie's spirit is a bit restless. Seen any ghosts?"

"No self-respecting ghost would live in those conditions. Only person I've seen in the area—besides you, of course—was a black man. Fishing."

I couldn't resist.

"What did the fisherman look like?"

"Old, thin, and wiry. Why?"

"Nothing, really. Did you ride your motorbike over here? I didn't hear an engine."

"Actually, it's an easy, if very damp, walk from there to here. Once you've crossed the bridge, there's a path. It's muddy, what with the river lapping at its edge. But it's a bit of a lark hiking in warm weather and not having some sniper looking on."

He would think that.

"Be careful, John. This isn't the English countryside. Among other things, *this* perimeter has venom and fangs."

"I remembered from last time and came prepared."

He pulled a penlight from his pocket and briefly spotlighted a pair of thick-soled leather boots. What little leather I could see beneath the red mud was pebble-grained and golden brown.

He flicked off the light.

"Bullhide lacers. The salesgirl at the Western shop assured me that all the cowboys love them."

I responded to the hint of self-mockery in his voice.

"So, naturally, you bought them."

"Naturally. Right after she convinced me they were impervious to snake bites."

I laughed, then said: "Unfortunately, the problem involves a bit more than the occasional wandering reptile. There's someone out there who seems to enjoy leaving venomous snakes in unexpected places."

I told him about Alex's stalker.

"Nasty," he said. "Callaghan strikes me as the consummate team player. I'd think he'd have every cop in Savannah—every cop in Chatham County—on alert."

I nodded.

"You should have seen them when Alex was shot. They swarmed like angry bees, pursued every lead, furious that someone dared strike at one of their own. Tommy thinks *that* fellow actually ended up in prison in Miami. Unrelated charges. But he wouldn't admit to the shooting. He died in a knife fight right around the time I left for London."

"Callaghan must have his reasons for protecting the stalker." His voice made it a question.

"Damned if I know what they are. Though he *did* make it clear that he'd arrange for protection for me in a heartbeat. I'm thinking it might be a good idea to take him up on his offer."

"That would certainly make my job easier."

I lit another cigarette off the end of my old one, spent a few minutes smoking, looking out at the fog, manipulating scenarios in my mind. Then I said: "*If* it's Sir William who's after me—and Mac seems to think it is—do you think he's the type to do the job personally?"

"Probably not. No way to know. What are you thinking, Jane?"

"Let's make Joey's innocent phone call work *for* us. Make this location work for us. It's familiar territory, unpopulated, and the environment is relatively easy to control. Certainly it's safer for me to take a stand here than to risk being ambushed on some busy London street. There's a good chance we can take out *whoever* is behind all of this."

Beside me, John shifted. I turned my head in his direction. His elbows were on his knees and, as he spoke, his attention remained on the ground between his feet.

"Dangerous," he said. "You're better off enlisting the police and getting some numbers on your side. I can't watch your back around the clock."

"I'll see what I can do. In the meantime, I'll stay close to the house. You stay at the bait shop, concentrate on the road. For anyone unfamiliar with the area, that bridge provides the only practical access to Alex's place. Even the locals won't risk the river when it's this high."

John agreed, sat up straight, faced me.

"So, any progress in the memory department?"

Obviously, Mac had seen fit to give John specifics about my situation. I tensed, certain that he'd also been instructed to probe for details and wondering what John's involvement would cost me.

I butted my cigarette and shredded it before answering.

"I've remembered a few things," I said warily. "Alex is helping me."

John surprised me by changing the subject.

"By the way, do you have a weapon?"

My shoulder muscles relaxed.

"No. I traveled light. Though, given the circumstances, that situation needs to be remedied. Soon."

"I thought that might be the case. The fellow with the Harley had some other merchandise for sale."

He opened his canvas bag, pulled out a revolver. A Colt Cobra. With its snub-nosed, two-inch barrel, it was easy to conceal, yet possessed considerable stopping power within an eight-meter range. It was a good defensive weapon.

I took it from him, spent a moment looking it over, touched the side latch, swung out the cylinder chamber. Empty.

I looked at John.

"Ammo?"

He dug around in the bag again, eventually came up with a box of .38 Special cartridges. Before handing them to me, he started to say something, then glanced in the direction of the Colt, stopped speaking, and frowned.

I followed the direction of his gaze, realized that John's eyes were well adjusted to the dark and that he could see I was supporting my weak right arm with my left hand. I let go, held my left hand out, palm up, and gestured with my fingers for him to give me the box.

"It's no good without bullets."

"You think you can manage to load it?"

He sounded worried.

I chose to misinterpret the question.

"It's been a while since I've used a revolver, but if I remember correctly . . . One bullet at a time, isn't it?"

He laughed.

The sound of a car turning on to the property brought our conversation to an end. John stood hurriedly.

"Time to rush back to my shack for dinner. I do so love MREs, particularly the pork chow mein."

I made a sympathetic noise. Though they were lightweight, bug- and rodent-proof, and required no refrigeration, Meals, Ready-to-Eat were notoriously unpalatable. American soldiers, for whom the rations were developed, had nicknamed them "Meals, Rejected by Everyone."

John lingered for a moment longer, rattled off a cell phone number, then opened the canvas bag he carried and handed me four black boxes. They were small enough that I could have closed my hand comfortably around any one of them.

"If you need help, just call. If I see anyone suspicious, I'll phone, then follow them."

He turned, walked across the drive, and disappeared into the fog.

I shoved the crystal-controlled room bugs into the pocket with my cigarettes and lighter and hurried up the front steps, already considering the best spots to plant them. John and I had used ones like them on other assignments. They had a transmitting range of about a mile, excellent sound quality, and tiny lithium batteries that were reliable for about five days.

I paused as I reached the door, confirming that the approaching car was, indeed, Alex's. He drove past the house, low beams on, his speed suggesting familiarity rather than caution. The fog eddied and swirled around the fast-moving car, reflected the red glow of the brake lights as Alex stopped in front of the carport.

I didn't wait to see the brake lights go off.

I turned, put my hand on the doorknob—

Gasped.

A rattlesnake's severed head was tacked over the knocker on the front door. Mouth open, fangs extended, eyes sunken. There were smears of blood across the white door.

I went inside, locked the door carefully, rearmed the alarm, and went into the library. I put the revolver, bullets, and listening devices into my purse.

I was still wearing Alex's coat when I went into the kitchen and opened the back door for him.

He smiled when he saw me, shifting the brown paper sack he carried into the crook of his left arm and putting his other arm around my shoulders. Our lips met, and casual greeting slipped into enthusiasm.

After a time, he noticed my coat.

"I went out front to smoke a cigarette and found another souvenir."

I showed Alex the front door.

The blood streaks spelled the word "die."

"This is classic, and you know it," I said as he stared at the door. "Your stalker is working himself up. He's no longer relying on fate—God, if you will—to deliver a death blow. He's becoming more violent, losing his inhibition about shedding blood. Call for help, Alex."

He shook his head, murmured: "That's not like him. Not like him at all."

"Not like whom?"

He shook his head again.

"Let's eat, before dinner gets cold."

21

Dinner was from Morrison's Cafeteria on Bull Street—fried chicken, turnip greens, and corn bread, with egg-custard pie for dessert. Afterward, Alex went upstairs to change into civvies. By the time he returned to the first floor, I had planted John's bugs. Kitchen. Foyer. Upstairs hallway. Verandah.

I had poured myself a Scotch and was in the library, sitting in front of the computer. I called out to him, invited him to join me, patted the chair next to mine.

As he sat down, I double-clicked on the document called "Jane."

"This is what happened," I said. "This is what I clearly remember. There's more, but it's too fragmented. Too unreliable."

I turned the screen toward him.

He read the document slowly, scrolling down to read the second page. Then he moved the cursor back to the beginning and reread it.

"Jesus Christ, Jane," he whispered finally, his eyes still on the screen.

He turned toward me, looked as if he were about to cry for the child I had once been. And then he stood and held out his hand.

I lay on my back beneath the kitchen table.

A very peculiar place to be.

Alex lay beside me, his shoulder against mine.

The kitchen was dark, as was most of the first floor. Even the porch light was off, eliminating the usual glow through the eyelet curtains on the back door. The only light in the room was the eerie green glow of the LCD display on the microwave oven. The luminous digits read 8:56 P.M.

Minutes earlier, I'd followed Alex from room to room, watching as he turned off the lights. He paused only once in his task, snatching a pair of throw pillows from the sofa in the living room. He handed those to me, then continued through the living room to the den, where he left a single lamp glowing. Its light wasn't visible from the kitchen.

He didn't volunteer any explanation, and I didn't ask questions, which made the trip through the first floor a study in silence.

His odd behavior continued into the kitchen, where he took a torch from the utility drawer, switched it on, then turned out the kitchen light. He used the torch's bright beam to guide our trip to the center of the room, then switched it off as—at his request—I ducked beneath the table.

"Comfortable?" he asked.

The kitchen was warm, the linoleum smooth and cool, and the pillow beneath my head and neck reasonably soft. So, really, I had no reason to complain.

"Uh-huh."

"Give me your hand."

He reached over, touched my arm, and followed it to my hand.

I attempted to interlock my fingers with his.

"No, like this," he said.

He wrapped his hand around mine. It was large, his fingers long. He easily encircled my wrist, engulfing most of my hand in his.

He was strong enough to restrain me if he wanted to.

I pulled my hand away, uncomfortable with the confinement.

My hand slid freely from beneath the weight of his.

He made no move to retrieve it.

"Please, Jane. I know it's hard for you. But try to trust me just a little."

I wanted to shout at him.

I wanted to say: What the hell more do you want? I've crawled beneath the fucking kitchen table with you. Isn't that enough?

But the very thought of those words inspired a bubble of laughter. I smothered the sound with the back of my hand. It emerged as a strangled hiccup.

Relax, I told myself. We'd shared a bed. We shared space beneath the kitchen table. Doubtful that holding hands could be any riskier.

I slipped my hand back into his.

"Good girl."

Briefly, he lifted my palm to his lips.

Then he switched on the torch, aiming it at the underside of the table. It was covered with writing—block printing, childish calligraphy, and occasionally an adult cursive I recognized as Alex's.

He turned off the flashlight before I could do more than glance at the messages. They were written with indelible marker and pencil and ink. Some were dated. Most were not. But each message began and ended the same way.

"Dear Mommy and Daddy."

"Love, Joey."

Alex nudged his body closer to mine and spoke quietly. His accent thickened, the way it always did when he spoke about family or feelings.

"It was a Sunday afternoon. I remember that because Joey'd been home from the hospital just two days, and a couple of ladies from church stopped by to drop off some casserole dishes. After they left, I put the food in the fridge, then called Joey. I didn't get an answer, but she never wandered far, so I hollered up the stairs and out the back door. No answer.

"Then I happened to glance toward the center of the kitchen and saw one of the chairs shift. I looked under the table and found her. Sitting right here with all the chairs pulled in tight all around her. Not playing and not pretending, like I remembered she was always doing when she was real little. Just sitting and staring out. Like she was trapped in some kind of cage.

"And, God knows, I knew what that was like. The Vietcong favored cages for their prisoners. Bamboo cages so small you never for a moment forgot you were trapped, not even when you were sleeping. Once you'd hung there long enough, once you were hurting bad enough, you began thinking, 'I just don't want to be here anymore.' And you'd just kind of let yourself drift away. To someplace better. Somewhere it didn't hurt.

"Tommy and I, we got real drunk one night and talked about it. About the cages, and the VC, and the guys who didn't make it. Turned out that during the really bad times, we'd both imagined ourselves back here, playing Swamp Fox, drinking lemonade on the verandah. Thing is, neither of us ever really lost touch with reality. Maybe worrying about each other kept us coming back to those damned cages. Some of the guys, though, they just, well, escaped permanently. I remember the look . . ."

He went silent, and the hand around mine tightened briefly.

Some memories, I thought, were best left unvisited.

After a minute, I felt him shrug.

"So there I was, and there she was under the kitchen table, and I panicked. Damn it. I was maybe twenty-three years old and the only thing I'd ever done in my life was fight in 'Nam. I had no business taking care of a little girl. Especially one who'd been through what she had. But I knew if I didn't figure out the right thing to do, she'd end up in bad trouble. So I said a prayer, and I crawled under the table with her.

"It was about then I spotted the red pencil. I'd been balancing the checkbook the night before, and the pencil probably just rolled off the table. I don't know why I picked it up, but I did. And then, more to have something to say than because I had a coherent plan, I said to her, 'Maybe we should write Mommy and Daddy a letter.' Joey looked at me with those big solemn eyes of hers and said, 'Cain't. Don't have any paper. And the postman doesn't deliver mail to heaven.' That's when I thought of this."

He turned on the torch again, shined it upward.

"I told her that the table was magic, and Mommy and Daddy'd be able to read anything she wrote here. For the next few months, she wrote a lot of letters. I wrote a few myself. Even years later, I'd occasionally find her here. She'd grin up at me, say 'Just visiting,' and invite me to join her."

He let go of my hand, gave me the torch.

Mostly to please him, I aimed the light randomly at one message, then another. I quickly found myself engrossed in a little girl's feelings, a little girl's thoughts.

'I miss you. Why'd you have to go and die like that?'

'I hate Alex. He made me eat spinach.'

'Will Santa Claus still know what I want for Christmas?'

'I punched Bobby Simms because he said Alex was a pig.'

'Mrs. Greene is the meanest teacher in the whole school.'

'Alex says that when parakeets die, they go to heaven, too.'

After a few minutes, Alex wrapped his fingers lightly around my wrist and guided the beam of the torch to a far corner.

It spotlighted a sentence that was printed in bold red marker.

I stared at it.

Inside my head, I heard a child's voice asking that very question. English accent. Not wistful or unhappy. Angry and aggressive.

Just like the red letters printed on the underside of the table.

'Why didn't I die, too?'

I yanked my hand away from Alex's, rolled onto my side, put the torch down so its beam illuminated nothing more than the kitchen floor.

It was long past time to get out from under the frigging table.

"I need a cigarette."

I made the words a challenge, made it clear that I would fight him if he tried to stop me. Then I sat up, taking care not to bang my head.

Alex didn't touch me.

"Funny," he drawled. "Never figured you for a coward."

I hated him, hated his perceptions.

"Damn you," I said.

But I lay back down.

Alex spoke quietly, his tone coaxing.

"Why didn't you die, too, Jane?"

I was still angry.

"If I could remember that, I wouldn't be here, would I?"

He repeated the question.

Fucking cop.

I didn't answer him.

The kitchen was dark.

The linoleum was hard and cold.

The room was silent, except for the ticking of the damned clock. It hung above the kitchen sink—a black cat with a clock for a belly and green rhinestone eyes that moved in opposition to its tail.

I pressed my lips together tight, imagined the cat's glittering green eyes moving back and forth, back and forth, as it marked the seconds. Childish stubbornness, but that's how I felt.

"Why didn't you die, too, Jane?"

I finally answered him just so he'd quit asking.

"I don't remember."

"You remember being dragged from the car."

A statement, but I answered it anyway.

"Yes."

"And you remember looking up at a gun."

"Yes."

"What kind of gun was it?"

No one else had ever asked me that. Why would they?

The scene flashed to mind again.

Olive trees. The afternoon sun hanging in a cloudless sky. Rocky dry earth beneath my knees.

I looked up at the masked man.

The sun outlined his figure in light, haloed his head, cast his face in shadow.

He pointed his gun.

I stared into its muzzle.

I was going to die.

The scene shifted.

Or, rather, the way I viewed the scene shifted.

For the first time, I looked at the gun, not the dark hole at the end of its barrel.

Fear forgotten, I sought details of the weapon with adult expertise.

I measured the size of the gun relative to the shooter's hand.

I saw a magazine-fed semiautomatic of World War II vintage and a one-piece wraparound walnut grip.

I noticed a safety lever on the left side, convenient to a right-handed shooter's thumb.

"A Mauser 1934."

Surprise in my voice.

Alex didn't give me time to think about it.

"Did the man in the mask have his finger on the trigger?"

"Yes."

"And he'd fired before."

"Yes."

"How often?"

"Three times."

"Who did he shoot?"

"Mama. Papa. Stavros."

"Then he pointed the Mauser at you."

"Yes."

"And it jammed."

Without really thinking, I shook my head.

"No, that's not what happened."

"Why didn't he shoot you, Jane?"

I blurted out the answer I didn't know I had.

"Because the other man wouldn't let him."

Alex stopped asking questions.

Hardly daring to breathe, I considered what I said. And another piece of my childhood fell into place. I sought Alex's hand with mine, tucked my fingers beneath his. Only then did I feel safe enough to tell him what I remembered.

I stared upward at the man holding the gun.

He'd shot Papa and Mama and Stavros. Now he would shoot me.

"Sorry, love. You weren't supposed to be here."

He was interrupted by a shout.

"No! Not the child."

The man sounded British, like the gunman, like my parents, like most of the people in the embassy compound.

I turned my head toward this new voice.

The Mercedes that made us crash was now parked on the other side of the road. The man who had just spoken stood beside it. Like the gunman, he was dressed in the rough, dark clothing of a Greek peasant and wore a stocking mask.

The gunman kept the Mauser pointed at me.

"You said no witnesses."

"She's a child."

I stayed very quiet, waiting for them to decide.

Maybe they'd forget I was there.

My stomach hurt.

The man with the gun shrugged, moved the gun closer to my head.

"Children listen. Children talk."

The second man lifted his chin in the direction of our car, then stared down at me through the ragged holes cut in the mask. His eyes were light brown flecked with yellow.

"Those two are a political problem, something for the British to handle. And the driver? A Greek, yes. But not an important man. And not from this area. The locals will investigate, but soon they'll be distracted by other matters. But if you kill a little girl . . . We'll have British intelligence after us. *And* the bloody Greeks. You know how they are where children are concerned. Sentimental fools. They'll be outraged. And persistent."

Overhead, the kitchen lights were on.

The digits on the microwave read 10:30 P.M.

The cat clock moved its glittery green eyes and swung its tail to mark the seconds.

Alex and I sat *at* the table, drinking coffee.

Back to normal, I thought. Except now I knew. That was assuming I could trust what I remembered. Once again, I wondered how much was fact and how much was imagination? How much had the nasty little drug session with Mac influenced my memory?

Good questions. No answers. Confirmation would come when Sir William tried to kill me. Then I would *really* know.

I made sure my voice was more confident when I spoke to Alex.

"There *is* one thing I'm now certain of. Mac isn't lying about

Sir William's involvement. It was him that day. The eyes were the same. Unmistakable."

Alex nodded, scooped sugar into his coffee, banged the spoon around inside the mug much longer than was necessary. Finally, he met my eyes and frowned.

"What's wrong?"

"There were *two* men, Jane. Sir William saved your life. Who the hell was the shooter?"

22

My arm cramped in the middle of the night.

I woke to muscles caught in violent spasm, muscles locked so tight that they no longer seemed to be made of flesh. I sat up in bed, bit my lip to keep from crying out.

Beside me, Alex was asleep.

I hugged my right arm to me, kneading the biceps with my left hand, waiting for the spasm to pass. Eventually my muscles relaxed and knotted cords became pliable.

Released from pain, I closed my eyes, exhaled, and continued cradling my right arm with my left. I concentrated on breathing, on relaxing, on trusting my body not to betray me again. It took me a few minutes to work up the courage to move my arm. I began by wiggling my fingers, built confidence by clenching and unclenching my fist and flexing my wrist. I risked extending my arm, then straightened my elbow.

The muscles locked up.

I whimpered, grabbed my arm, held it close, bent my body over it.

"Let me help," Alex said.

I didn't know that I'd awakened him, hadn't noticed him sitting up in bed. But he seemed to know what was wrong.

He ran warm, strong fingers down my right arm, pushed my left hand away from my biceps. He massaged my arm slowly, beginning at a point just below my shoulder, ending at the elbow, increasing pressure as my arm relaxed beneath his hands.

I let out a long sigh as the pain diminished. Then I tried to move my arm.

Alex stopped me.

"Stay still," he said. "Give the muscles a chance to recover."

He supported my elbow with one hand as he shifted so that he was sitting with his back against the headboard.

"Here. Lean against me. Try to sleep."

I did as he said, felt the warmth of his bare chest against my naked back, realized how chilled I was.

He slid his right arm around me so that it supported the length of my arm, caught the edge of the blanket with his other hand, and pulled it up around me. He put his left arm on top of the blanket and held me that way.

Naked, warm, and protected, I drifted to sleep.

I dreamt that the kitchen table stood in the midst of an olive grove. I was on hands and knees beneath it. Four chairs were pushed in around the table. Three were occupied by men who sat frozen, unmoving, unspeaking. I recognized their trouser legs and their shoes. Sir William. John. Mac.

All around the table, the twisted trunks of the olive trees grew up from the sun-dappled earth, their twisted branches clawing at a brilliant blue sky. In the distance, birds sang. A gentle wind rustled the leaves and carried the smell of petrol to my hiding place.

I knelt there, listening, not making a sound, ignoring the legs and feet that shared the space with me. I peered out between the tubular chrome legs of the single empty chair, looked down between the rows of trees, and watched the road.

Two cars were there.

The white one was off the road. It had crashed among the trees. Broken branches covered its hood, lay across the windshield. The front passenger-side door was open. And inside the car—

Even my dream mind sheered away from what was inside.

I looked instead at the man standing beside the car.

He wore a mask and, though I couldn't see it, I knew he had a gun. A Mauser 1934 with a walnut stock. He was holding a lighter to a long piece of cloth that hung from the gas tank. The cloth was streaked with furniture stain—dark walnut for the wardrobe in the guest suite, golden oak for the furniture in the bedroom.

Flames shot up the length of the cloth.

The man in the mask ran to the roadside. A battered black Mercedes waited there, its motor running, smoky exhaust pouring from its tailpipe. He slid in next to the driver.

The Mercedes pulled onto the road, then roared away, leaving a cloud of dust and exhaust in its wake.

The white car exploded.

Thick, black smoke boiled up into the cloudless sky.

I cowered beneath the table as chunks of metal rained

all around me, crashing through the tree branches, clattering against the tabletop.

Something warm and wet dropped onto my shoulder.

I turned my head, watched as a blob of crimson oozed down my bare arm, tickling me on its journey to my hand.

Where had that come from?

I sat back on my heels, tipped my head, looked upward.

Above me was a message scrawled in thick red liquid.

Why didn't you die, Jane?

It oozed and crawled across the underside of the table, dripped onto my face, my arms, my bare legs. Huge droplets splashed the white sundress I wore and spread darkly across my skirt.

A deep, drawling male voice spoke close to my ear.

"Let me help."

Startled, I turned my head.

Alex was there beside me, within the circle of legs and chairs. He sat with his legs folded, one of his knees touching one of mine.

He was dressed just like Stavros.

The bill of his chauffeur's cap was black and shiny, his starched shirt was spotlessly white, the creases in his slacks were sharp. His boots were polished and the thin spaghetti laces were neatly tied.

A cigarette hung from the corner of his mouth.

I was horrified to see him smoking. Hadn't he just been released from hospital? I clearly remembered a doctor's grim face and the words *tension pneumo*. I couldn't recall what it meant.

"I'm certain that can kill you," I said.

He shook his head, took a long drag, used two fingers

to lift the cigarette from his lips. He smiled, offered it to me.

I took the cigarette, inhaled deeply. Then I put it out on the ground beside me.

"I don't want you to die."

Alex shook his head, laughed.

"Vietnam didn't kill me. Neither did that bullet. We live and die at the whim of Atropos."

He pulled a knife from his belt. Marine Corps issue KA-1217. Black single blade, half a foot long.

"Don't you remember the Parcae?" he said. "Clotho holds the wool. Lachesis spins the thread of life. And Atropos——"

He laid the razor edge against his leg, just above his boot, and sliced downward.

"——cuts it."

I cried out, wrenched awake.

Woke up in Alex's arms.

He held me tight, called my name, told me it would be all right.

I didn't believe him.

23

Dawn came, as it inevitably does, and pushed away the horrors of the night. I turned off the alarm a full hour before it was set to ring, slipped from beneath the blankets, and left the bed where I had lain sleepless for hours.

Alex was snoring softly into the pillows, body oriented toward the center of the bed, an arm outstretched across the blankets as if he were still holding me.

It was absurd to stand beside the bed like a character in some silly romance, my eyes lingering over my lover's lean cheeks and long lashes and sensuous lips. I didn't need to watch him sleeping, didn't want to be reminded of his passion or his kindness or his little-boy sweetness. Or of the words he'd whispered when he thought I was asleep.

I didn't care that he loved me.

When this was over, I would leave Savannah. Leave him behind.

That was easy enough to do when you were an exemplary

undercover operative. Mac had once described me that way, proudly claiming me as one of his best creations.

Given a role, I could become it.

Given an environment, I could adapt to it.

Given a situation, I could manipulate it.

Then I could walk away, casting off the latest alter ego, discarding irrelevant experiences, and suppressing disruptive emotions. Like a snake shedding its skin.

Given a few weeks to recover, I could repeat the cycle again.

And again.

And again.

I'd worked in Britain, Ireland, Canada, Australia, the States. I'd been a factory worker, a college student, a terrorist, a drug smuggler, an escaped criminal. They'd called me Molly Shanks and Morgana Keast and Moura McCarthy and so many other names I could hardly remember them.

Mac's exemplary undercover operative.

Until I'd quit.

Coming to Savannah last spring was my idea. The experiences and emotions of the past ten months didn't belong to some alter ego conceived to serve Mac's requirements. They belonged to Jane Nichols.

If I ran away from her, then who the hell would be left?

I turned my back on Alex, refocused my attention on dressing in a pair of jeans and an oversized white shirt. Then I slipped on a pair of running shoes and concentrated on keeping the tension even as I pulled the laces tight. The bows were easy, and the laces didn't break. When I'd finished tying them, I straightened, glanced at my feet, and congratulated myself on this proof of growing self-sufficiency.

Small victories.

I walked down the back staircase, stopped at the base of the stairs, and looked into the kitchen.

Not unexpectedly, the table was in the center of the room, just where it belonged. No one was sitting at the chairs. They were neatly tucked in, just as Alex and I had left them the night before.

A shaft of sunlight crept in between the curtains on the back door, slanting across the glossy floor. But the light hadn't yet reached the table and chairs. The space under the table was in deep shadow. I lingered at the edge of the kitchen with my hand on the light switch, loath to cross the room, afraid of what might be lurking there.

A damned stupid reaction to a kitchen table.

Get over it, Nichols, I told myself.

I left the light off, stalked over to the table, pulled out a chair, and sat down. I put my elbows on the table and my legs beneath it. I waited.

No one hacked off my foot with a big knife.

No one dropped an amputated foot into my lap.

The sound of shattering glass, of metal against metal wrenched me to my feet.

I ran.

Outside.

Out through the back door.

Around to the front of the house.

Alex's squad car was in the driveway.

Its right front fender was smashed, as was its right headlight.

There was blood on all the windows.

Smeared across the windows.

Dripping down the windows.

I screamed.

I didn't want to see—

*　　*　　*

Blood. It spattered the glass, ran down it in rivulets.

So at first I couldn't see—

Two crumpled bodies in the backseat. Covered in blood. Gaping flesh where faces had once—

Mama!

Papa!

I screamed.

I didn't *want* to see.

I threw myself backward, fighting his grasp, fighting to break free. He caught the back of my dress, spun me around, slammed me against the car. He pulled open the rear door, forced me inside, forced me against the still warm—

I clawed my way out.

"Jane! Come back!"

Alex was holding on to me. Shaking me. Standing between me and the car. Blocking my view. Alex, wrenched from sleep, wearing only his boxers, holding his service revolver.

"It's okay, Jane. You're here. Now. Safe."

I looked up into his face, refocused on the present, on someone else who would leave me—

"You'll die, too."

He put his left arm around me. Pulled me to him.

"No, honey. That won't happen. Not for a lot of years."

The scar on his chest reminded me he was lying.

I wanted to run.

But his body was warm. So nice and warm. And safe.

I wanted to cry. I wanted to tell him—

I caught the inside of my lip between my teeth, bit down hard.

"I know a flashback when I see it," he was saying. "Tommy and I—"

He took a deep breath, hugged me closer.

"Do you want to tell me about it?"

I shook my head, straightened, and stepped away.

He let me go.

I walked to the squad car and forced myself to look at it closely.

A large snake. Hacked to pieces. Strewn and smeared on the squad car's windows.

Inside the carport, the Blazer was unscathed.

I turned on my heel, confronted Alex.

"How long are you going to let this go on?"

He rubbed the scar on his forehead.

"Another day or two. No more. I swear."

By ten o'clock, the clouds had chased the sun away. The overcast chilled the air. Though it wasn't raining, dampness crept quickly through the house.

The phone rang.

Alex answered it, and I listened to his half of the conversation.

"No, Pumpkin."

"Jane's a bit under the weather. Maybe a touch of flu."

"Can we have dinner with you in a few days?"

"No, no. No need to come out here."

"Yes? Okay. I'll tell her."

He hung up the phone and raised an eyebrow in my direction.

"Joey says thanks, she owes you."

Alex wasn't the only one capable of a blank expression and no response.

I retreated to the library, turned on all the lamps and the gas fireplace, sat at my computer. I thought about Alex's stalker and decided that the problem needed to be resolved. Soon. I spent some time considering how best to do it.

Alex pulled on a sweatshirt inside out, over a T-shirt and old, soft jeans, and roamed around the house doing odd jobs. He started outside, took a scrub brush and soapy water with him. I heard the brush scrape the front door, knew the squad car was next. I wondered how he'd explain this *incident* to Tommy.

The day passed slowly.

Every now and again, Alex would smile or wave in my direction as he passed though the foyer carrying an overflowing wastebasket or a stack of clean towels or a bottle of glass cleaner and a wad of newspaper.

Neither of us seemed in the mood to talk.

We were tired, I thought. Physically and emotionally.

Andrew Jax was a welcome change from a man I couldn't control.

The words flowed easily onto the page. I typed several pages, rearranged several paragraphs, read the results, tinkered for a few minutes more, and was vaguely pleased.

> *The punk deserved to die.*
>
> *Jax held Marty Morris's head under the deep water in the bathtub and told himself just that.*
>
> *Marty struggled, kicked out with his five-hundred-dollar Gucci shoes. Air bubbles broke the water's surface.*
>
> *Jax laughed, jammed his toe into the back of Morris's knee, and shoved him in deeper.*
>
> *More bubbles. Larger this time.*
>
> *"Die, motherfucker. Die."*

"Andy, stop it!"

Millie stormed into the bathroom, grabbed his arm, yanked upward. Morris's head broke the surface. He took a deep, wheezing breath in the time it took Jax to shake Millicent off.

"Get out of here, Millie. Get out now!"

She stomped her foot, her spike heel against the tile floor snapping out her defiance.

"Screw you, Andrew Jax. I'm not leaving. You kill him, you'll have to do it in front of me."

Jax lifted Morris by the collar. He hung limp, like a drowned cat. Gulped air. Enjoy it, Jax thought as he turned toward Millicent, 'cause it's the last air you're going to get. Unless they serve oxygen in hell.

"This creep beat you up. Tried to rape you. Why the fuck do you care what happens to him?"

"Because we're friends."

"You and him?"

That was something Jax hadn't figured on.

"No, you jerk. Me and you."

Jax blinked once, twice, genuinely surprised.

Millicent frowned.

"Or at least, I think we're friends. We've been through a lot together—— Andy, do you trust me?"

Jax didn't answer.

Millicent leaned against the doorjamb, crossed her arms over her ample breasts.

"Decide. If you trust me, call the cops. Let them lock him up."

Jax looked at Millicent for a long time. For a change, Marty Morris had nothing to say. That made deciding easier. Jax dropped him. Kicked him in the balls just to make a point.

"Move, fucker," he said, "and I'll drown you in the toilet."

✳ ✳ ✳

I saved the file, dragged it to a folder entitled "Jax Too." Before long, I hoped, I would come up with a more creative title for book number five. I spent a few minutes considering the problem, came up with *Cracker Jax* and a subtitle: *Crazy After All These Years.* I decided it probably wouldn't do.

I got up and wandered into the kitchen, where I fixed ham and Swiss cheese sandwiches on rye for two. Alex ate his at the kitchen table while he read a week's accumulation of newspapers. I ate in front of the computer.

After that, Alex spent several hours in the first-floor bathroom, repairing a leak beneath the sink. I wrote a dozen letters—short, handwritten notes to readers who had written to me care of the publisher. My arm ached. Between letters, I stretched, listened to Alex work, and jotted down a few of his expletives, intending to eventually work them into Andrew Jax's dialogue.

We ate shrimp pie, salad, and warm, crusty French bread for dinner.

That night, we made love.

I snuggled in beside Alex, lingered in bed until his breathing was deep and regular, then slipped from his relaxed embrace. I dressed in jeans, a dark shirt, and boots, then detoured to the library to retrieve the drover's coat. With the Colt Cobra tucked into one of the deep pockets, I crept out the back door.

It was cool and dry and the wind was still.

A good night for hunting.

I hugged the shadows, crept around the house, and spent a few minutes surveying the grounds and the carport for wayward reptiles and a violent stalker. Nothing turned up, so I settled down in the deepest shadows beside the front steps and waited.

The chances were good that Alex's stalker would be back

tonight. Unless he'd struck while we were making love, he hadn't yet left today's token of his growing hatred, his escalating violence. I'd been watching. So, I could tell, had Alex.

I didn't smoke.

By two in the morning, my desire for nicotine was eclipsed by my need for caffeine. Five minutes after that, I heard a noise. Adrenaline brought wakefulness and a return of energy.

I pulled the gun from my pocket, peered out into the darkness, in the direction of the sound.

Someone was in the carport, I thought.

I waited.

A shadowy figure made its way across the yard.

I waited until he crept past me, then followed him noiselessly as he moved up the stairs. He carried an ax. One that was large enough to chop logs. Or snakes. Or a police chief.

When we reached the verandah, I stood behind one of the huge columns supporting the balcony and leveled my gun at his back.

Then he surprised me.

He marched to the front door, banged against it with the ax handle, and yelled at the top of his lungs.

"Chief! Please! Hurry! I need your help."

I hesitated, recognizing the voice.

The porch light switched on, and I saw the face that belonged to the voice. It was an old man's face. The face of the grizzled black man who drove me from the airport, who worried about his children and grandchildren and great-grandchildren, who told me about Willie's ghost.

Perhaps he was in trouble.

Perhaps his cab was stranded nearby.

He lifted the ax above his head, ready to strike when the door opened.

I aimed carefully, using my left hand to support my right.

Alex didn't come to the front door.

He stepped through the French doors from the living room. He emerged from the shadows fully dressed.

Apparently he'd been watching and waiting, too.

"Jane!" he said urgently. "Leave him be!"

I relaxed my grip, but kept my weapon ready.

Alex stood warily, out of ax range, watching the old man.

The cabby's eyes were fixed on him. As if no other threat existed. As if no other person existed.

The ax remained poised.

"What can I do for you, Sam?"

"My boy died in prison. Your fault."

Alex's hands were at his sides and surprisingly empty. Where the hell was his gun? He turned his hands palms out. Shrugged his shoulders. Kept his tone low and soothing.

"I didn't have anything to do with that, Sam. That was in Florida. Remember?"

Sam began shaking his head, back and forth, back and forth.

The head of the ax moved, too, catching the light on a newly honed edge.

Sam's voice was shrill, the cords on his neck bulging with tension.

"No! Your fault. He jus' wanted to scare you. He didn't aim at you. He tol' me that. You stepped right into that bullet. Then all those police came 'round asking questions. You made him run away."

The old man lunged forward, swung the ax in a wide arch.

Alex dove past him, rolled, came back up on his feet.

Sam whipped around him, screeching.

"You chased him away. Away from his family. Away from his daddy."

Each sentence was punctuated by another swing of the heavy ax.

Alex crouched, kept his center of gravity low, and kept moving. He backed down the length of the verandah. Buying time.

He must have phoned for help, I thought.

The relentless swings continued, the old man's appalling strength borne of insanity.

If Alex miscalculated, if one of the blows connected . . .

It was foolish to wait.

I had a clear shot at Sam's back.

I raised my gun again.

Alex saw me over Sam's shoulder. He shouted as he dodged the blade.

"Jane! No!"

A stubborn man.

It had to be his way.

I put the gun into my pocket and launched myself at Sam, driving my shoulder into the back of his knees.

I brought him down.

Later, rotating Mars lights swept the scene, blue strobes reflecting off the ax in a young policewoman's hands, off the sadness in Alex's face, off the tears rolling down an old man's cheeks.

"My job to protect him," Sam kept sobbing. "My job. My job. My job."

John phoned before the last squad car left.

Alex called me to the phone, then went back out to the driveway. As usual, he asked no questions.

"Your stalker?" John said.

"Yes."

"Your cop has good technique. I'll lay you ten-to-one he could have managed without you."

"That wasn't something I wanted to risk. You saw the whole thing?"

"Uh-huh. The old fellow parked his cab right on the bridge. The police are looking at it now, and the tow truck has just arrived. Anyway, the old man got out and opened the trunk. At first, I thought he was doing some night fishing. Then he pulled out the ax and a burlap sack. He went to the path by the river without hesitating. As if he'd walked it every day. I thought I'd do well to follow him. Then I saw you and stopped worrying."

"Thank you, ever so."

He chuckled and hung up.

24

I fell asleep on the sofa.

Fully dressed.

Alex woke me before dawn. He pulled me awake with a voice that held no urgency and kept me awake by stroking my cheek.

"Jane. Come on, honey. Open your eyes."

I pushed his hand away. I didn't want to wake up.

That didn't seem to matter to Alex.

"Come on, sleepyhead."

Why did he persist in sounding so obnoxiously cheerful?

I struggled into an upright position, pulling the afghan with me, half-opened my eyes. I noticed that it was still very dark outside and glanced at the clock.

Two hours.

I'd been asleep for only two hours.

Alex pushed a mug of coffee into my right hand and held it there long enough to make sure I had hold of it. Before I could shove it back at him, he moved to stand by the far end of the sofa.

Out of range. Clever man.

"Have your coffee. Then get up."

"Why?"

"We're going fishing."

I considered several retorts, contented myself with waving in the direction of the bedroom door, and using an appropriate Americanism.

"Go for it."

He tugged the afghan away from me.

I glared at him, saw that he was clean shaven, his dark hair was neatly combed, and he was dressed. A flannel shirt the color of mustard powder topped a pair of black jeans. Sexy. If I'd been in the mood.

He didn't go away.

"I said, '*We're* going fishing.' Everything's packed up, ready to go. Except for you and the night crawlers. Figured you could help me dig a few dozen from the compost heap."

"Fuck. You."

He laughed, stepped closer, ran a finger along the rise of my breasts.

"Later. Maybe. In the meantime, you have five minutes. Then I'm coming back with a container full of worms. If you're not up and moving . . ."

He left the threat hanging, smiled again—cheerfully, of course—and walked from the room. Then he poked his head back around the corner.

"Pull on a jacket. The temperature's dropped to about forty. And it's windy."

"Okay," I muttered.

Then I remembered that I'd heard Sam in the carport and that John had mentioned he carried a burlap sack.

"Please, Alex! Check for snakes!"

His smile wasn't quite so cheerful as the last one. Definitely forced.

"I already have. Apparently, he wasn't sure he'd get me with the ax. He left two pygmy rattlers inside the Blazer. I guess *that* lock was easy to open. I dumped 'em out back, off the path."

Fifteen minutes later, I was sitting beside Alex in the front seat of the Blazer dressed in yesterday's jeans, a clean black-and-white-plaid shirt, a jacket, and a pair of boots. On the floor beside my feet was my purse. Inside, the Colt Cobra was loaded.

As I'd retrieved my purse from the study, I'd asked Alex where we were going. Whether John was listening or, more likely, would review the tapes at a more civilized hour, he would have the information he needed. And I saw no risk in a fishing trip.

"Just down the road to the bridge by Willie's place," Alex said.

Alex backed the Blazer out of the carport.

I clipped on my seat belt and huddled into my jacket.

"You might want to hang on to the bait," he said.

I ignored his suggestion, left the used Styrofoam coffee cup filled with worms on the truck's broad dashboard. It had a lid. No need to cosset the squirming creatures trapped inside.

Then we hit a bump.

The cup bounced upward, dislodging the lid. Another bump would likely send cold, slimy worms flying—

I placed a hand firmly over the lid and held the cup in my lap.

Alex grinned.

I muttered something extremely rude.

We drove through the darkness, out between the twin pillars, along the winding road. Within a matter of minutes, we crossed the bridge, and Alex pulled the Blazer onto the shoulder. He left the front and rear driver-side tires on the road, which gave the bench seat a steep downhill list.

"Sorry," Alex said. "This is the best spot to park, but the shoulder's still real soft. Be careful when you step down."

I slid out, closed the door, found myself standing in several inches of mud, cursed under my breath, then slogged around to join Alex at the tailgate. He pulled a tackle box and two fishing poles from the back of the truck, handed me one. We walked back to the middle of the bridge.

Squinting to see by the dim, pre-dawn light, I threaded a worm onto a fishing hook, leaned forward against the thick plank railing, and cast my line into the Ogeechee River. The wind took the line toward the center of the river, the current carrying the red-and-white bobber downstream.

I waited until Alex had cast out his line, then asked: "What are we fishing for?"

"Doesn't matter. Fishing is an excuse. Just watch the sky."

The sun rose, scorching the darkness between the trees, creating a spider web silhouette of intertwined branches across a blaze of sky. The river swept beneath us, glimmering with drops of reflected light, then transforming to liquid fire.

I stood entranced.

The sun moved upward. The world brightened. Details emerged. Magic faded.

I couldn't avoid understatement.

"Nice," I said. "Thanks."

"You're welcome."

I leaned forward, rested my elbows on the railing, watched water droplets glinting on the filament line, branches swaying in the wind, sunlight on the water, and the bobber bobbing with the ripples. I heard traffic noise. Past dawn and the distant sound of cars and trucks was a constant reminder that Savannah was expanding outward, new roads cutting through the marshes like greedy tentacles.

A log swept by. Body sized.

I watched it travel downstream, at first concerned that it would tangle our lines. Then, as it passed, I remembered the cabby's gossip.

"Willie, he died fishin' off this very bridge."

And Alex's words: "It was a sad day when I found him floating under that bridge."

I imagined the bridge blocked by the SPD's white squad cars and Chatham County's dark blue ones. And a coroner's wagon. I imagined Alex down on the bank, wading in the shallow water, helping to pull a horribly decomposed body from the river and zipping it into a black plastic body bag.

Would Alex still fish off the bridge?

Unlikely.

Would he watch the sun rise without at least mentioning his dear friend?

Never. He was far too sentimental.

I glanced at him. His eyes were on the water, and he was using the reel, slowly working his line back upstream. Relaxed. At peace.

Peculiar.

I made a guess. I kept my voice matter-of-fact and my eyes on the river as I voiced it.

"Willie's still alive, isn't he? You thought he was leaving the snakes."

25

The sun was warm.

Alex had taken off his jacket and rolled up the sleeves on his flannel shirt. He sat up on the railing, just inches from where I stood. His back was to the sun, his bare elbows on his knees.

I was still comfortable in my jacket. I left it on, continued fishing.

I kept my eyes on the bobber and the river. Anywhere but Alex's face. Every time I looked at him, he'd look down at the bait cup or the tackle box or simply stare at his feet.

I waited, not pushing, giving him time to think.

His lack of denial had already confirmed my guess.

Finally, he began speaking, sounding almost as if he were talking to himself.

"Since the day I met him, Willie told me about his dreams. They weren't real big by regular folk's measure. More like a series of wants than anything else. A new fishing pole. A new pair of shoes. A feather pillow. A wristwatch. He'd find himself a dream, and every bit of him would work to make it real. Then he'd find another one. As he got older, his dreams got bigger. But still, they were nothing more than most of us just take for granted. Or simply consider our due."

I felt a tug on the line.

Ignored it.

"So five, maybe six years ago, he dreamed of a house. Nothing big or fancy. Just a three-room frame ranch on high and dry ground. With a screened-in porch overlooking the river. He stopped by my place one evening, dropped off some peach preserves, and told me about it. I remember sayin' that if he sold off a bit of his land, he'd have enough money for his house and then some. He asked me if I'd ever sell *my* daddy's land. When I told him no, he said that was good. He said he figured that if folks like us kept selling off what we owned, there'd soon be nothing wild left. Everything would be covered by lawns and houses and pavement. Just like in town."

I glanced at Alex's face, saw nothing but pain.

I looked back at the river.

The bobber ducked beneath the surface.

Once. Twice.

Alex continued talking, his voice low, his drawl slowing his sentences and loading each word with emotion.

"So he decided to build the house himself. He figured to make extra money selling produce and peach preserves. I tried to help him, but he was proud and I was busy. But mostly, I think we'd just grown apart. What we'd shared was childhood, fishing, and hot summer days. And dreams. Those days were still real for Willie, but I'd left them behind. In Vietnam. In the wreck that took my parents. In the things I saw on the streets every day. I was raising Joey, watching her take joy in things I remembered loving. Some days, I swear, she was the only thing that kept me from curling up and dying."

One more tug at the line, and it went slack.

I'd lost my bait, I thought.

At the moment, it didn't matter.

Alex stopped speaking, half turned, and looked over his shoulder.

His deep, slow tone remained the same as he said: "That hook's been there awhile. Why don't you reel it on in? Let's make sure you still have some bait."

The abrupt change in topic was disconcerting. But I did as he said, ended up with the bobber and empty hook dangling from several feet of line.

Alex scooted himself off the railing, squatted down, and lifted the lid on the Styrofoam cup.

"Swing your hook over here. I'll bait it for you."

"I can do it myself. Really."

He tipped his face toward me.

"Of course you can. I wasn't challenging your competence, Jane. I never have."

He looked back at the cup, pulled out a worm, and held it up for my inspection.

"This one okay?"

It was a worm, like any other.

I didn't say so.

I nodded, then watched him slip the hook through it. When he was finished, I dropped the line back into the water.

Alex rigged his line again and stood beside me as he dropped it in the river.

Between us, there was a lot of quiet.

"What happened to Willie?" I said finally.

"We ended up as nothing more than neighbors who waved as our cars passed on the road home. So I didn't notice that all of a sudden, he had money. Seems he decided to try growing a cash crop on some of those high and dry acres of his. He really didn't see the harm. Figured growing marijuana was no worse than growing tobacco, and a lot easier on the land. Like so many things he put his hand to, he did it well.

"But dope isn't like vegetables. You can't sell a bumper crop from a roadside stand out in the middle of nowhere. The only way to get your crop to market is to get involved with people who are in the business of supplying all kinds of drugs. One shipment, one deal, and then *they've* got *you*. They've got your place, which is real remote. A real nice place to hide people and product."

Alex yanked the line with enough force to shake the bait off, reeled it in, shook his head, and propped the pole back against the rail. He rested his elbows on the rail beside mine and looked out at the river.

"Willie's *friend* had drifted away," he said. "But the *cop* who lived at the end of the road began noticing a little more traffic than usual, a little more business than usual at the bait shop. And though the friend hadn't bothered stopping by to visit in years, the cop came knocking at his door. By then, Willie was desperate to get out. I helped him cut a deal with the DEA. He testified against some real nasty people, and the Feds put him into the witness protection program. Found him a nice place. Somewhere else."

"What about the body?"

"An indigent who fell off a railroad bridge in Atlanta. No relatives. So the Feds shipped the body down here, and Tommy and I filed a report saying we fished it out from under *this* bridge. We gave the John Doe a real nice burial. And I figured we'd done all we could to keep Willie safe."

He turned his head, met my eyes, started to speak, and

abruptly looked away. He began talking in the direction of the river again.

"Problem is, Willie is too tied to his land to stay away very long. Lots of people have seen him, which is how the ghost story got started. Hell, *I've* seen him at least a dozen times over the past year. Usually at night, walking by the side of the road. I'll be driving past, spot him out of the corner of my eye. And every time, I've slammed on the brakes, turned the car around, and gone back to talk to him. But he always slips away, back into the marsh. I guess he doesn't want to talk to me. So when this started, I naturally figured—"

Abruptly, he stepped back from the railing, grabbed his pole, bent to pick up the tackle box and bait cup, then straightened.

"If you don't mind, let's get out of here."

His face was stiff, his voice thick, and he didn't wait for my reply.

He turned on his heel and walked to the back of the truck. After dropping the tailgate, he put the tackle box down on it and spent a moment dumping the worms into the wet grass beyond the road's soft shoulder.

I reeled in my line, but I didn't go to him right away.

I stood on the bridge, holding my pole, watched as he disassembled his rod and reel, violently yanking the pieces apart. He flung them into the back of the truck, stood with his back still to me.

"Damn it!" he said. "Damn it all to hell!"

I walked over to him then.

I stood behind him, brushed my fingers over his cheek and neck, then rested my hand on his shoulder. Someone, I thought, should tell him that he wasn't responsible for every life that touched his.

I said: "So you thought Willie had come back to punish you for doing your job. And for failing as a friend."

He nodded.

"Yeah. And because I have his land. I had no idea he'd go and leave it to me to take care of. But that's what his note said. And the paperwork was already filed. But he's had a couple years to think about it. I thought maybe he decided he'd made a mistake. Maybe he figured I *wanted* to take his daddy's land away from him."

It didn't matter where Willie was, I thought. His spectre remained in Savannah. Haunting Alex.

Guilt was like that.

Even irrational guilt.

Someone, I thought, should tell Alex.

Perhaps, someday, I would.

The distinctive crack and echo of a high-powered rifle interrupted his words and my thoughts. It preceded the bullet by a heartbeat.

Alex and I dove into the red mud behind the passenger side of the car, putting the truck between us and the shooter. The bullet slammed into the side of the tackle box, sent it tumbling, sent fish hooks and bobbers and lures spraying onto the road.

Our eyes met. Fear in his. Undoubtedly in mine, too.

"You have a gun?" I asked a little breathlessly.

He nodded.

"My backup. In the glove compartment. You?"

"Colt Cobra. In my purse. On the floor."

No surprise in Alex's expression. It wasn't the first time I'd carried a weapon along on an innocent outing.

I was nearest the door. I reached up, caught the handle, discovered there wasn't enough strength in my right hand to manage the latch from that angle.

Alex moved in close, grabbed the handle, and released the door. He let it swing open less than an inch, then hunkered down low. Encouraged by little more than gravity, the door swung open above our heads.

A bullet smashed in through the driver-side window and out through the open door. Another bullet followed the same path as the first, just a few inches lower, piercing the door panel, whizzing past us, embedding itself in a tree trunk.

Alex and I buried our faces in our arms.

When we dared lift our heads again, Alex said: "If that's a Lee-Enfield or the like—and I'd be willing to swear it was—and if the shooter is halfway competent—which he seems to be—then one of us is damned lucky not to be dead. I'm guessing it's you."

I didn't deny it.

His eyes were hard, the characteristic warmth gone from his expression. A reminder not to mistake compassion and decency for weakness. Or lack of courage.

"We've got to get out of here," he said. "First things first."

He took a deep breath, exhaled slowly, then slid in through the open door, flattening himself against the rubber mats. He snagged the purse with his left hand and shoved it back in my direction, along the left side of his body.

Part of the bulky purse dragged beneath the seat.

I grabbed the strap, tugged it free, immediately pulled out the Colt and released the safety.

Alex supported his body on his right arm, reached over his head with his left, and unlatched the glove compartment. He eased it open and retrieved a holstered semiautomatic. Then he pulled his hand away slowly, lowering his left arm nearly to the mat.

I heard a high-pitched buzz.

The two-foot-long rattlesnake struck at Alex with curved fangs.

Struck from beneath the front seat.

Hit him above his elbow. Once. Twice.

Alex yelped, dropped his gun, flinched away.

My shot paralleled the floor, dangerously close to Alex's body.

The bullet hit the snake, split it almost in half, then penetrated the floor where it bowed upward to accommodate the drive shaft.

Alex's face was pale and strained.

"A pygmy rattler. Not lethal. I swear."

His breathing came in quick, short gasps.

It was still cool outside, but beads of sweat were forming on his forehead. His elbow was already swelling, the skin just above it an ugly, ruddy purple and getting tighter by the moment. The puncture wounds were marked by thin trails of blood.

I needed to get him to hospital. Candler was only twenty minutes away. The route was burned into my memory.

"Keys?" I said.

He retrieved them from his trouser pocket, focusing all his attention on moving his hand those few inches.

I watched his face, regretting not getting the keys myself. I took them from him as quickly as I could. Then I tucked my purse and the Colt in beside him, pulled his SIG-Sauer from its holster and put it in my jacket pocket.

I crawled past him, keeping my head low and brushing sharp

cubes of safety glass from the driver's seat as I moved forward. I stuck the key in the ignition.

"Get into the truck," I said.

Alex crawled, trying not to groan, and wedged himself into the cab. He leaned against the seat, left arm up, his butt on the floor, legs tucked in, and knees pointing toward the gear shift. His breathing was getting worse, his complexion greying.

A crack, an echo, and then a bullet whizzed through the cab.

I kept my head below the level of the glassless side window, depressed the clutch with my left foot, and kept it there. I held the steering wheel with my left hand. With my right, I turned the key in the ignition.

The engine roared to life.

I threw the gearshift into first and released the hand brake.

My arm objected. I ignored it.

I pressed the accelerator with my right foot, released the clutch. As the truck lurched forward, I glanced over the steering wheel, then ducked again as a bullet whizzed past me.

I risked another look at the road, depressed the clutch again, and shifted to second. I accelerated to thirty miles per hour, then shifted to third.

Ahead of me, the road curved sharply.

I pressed the accelerator, taking advantage of the bit of straight road that still remained, and urged the truck to forty-five.

Briefly, I turned my head to check Alex.

He was pale and breathing open-mouthed, but he was still conscious.

He managed the ghost of a smile.

"Old-fashioned girl," he gasped.

Damn it! I didn't want to love him.

I returned my attention to the road, holding tight to the

steering wheel as the road curved left. I adjusted the steering to avoid a deep pothole and didn't quite manage.

The Blazer bucked beneath us, slowing fractionally.

A bullet whizzed past my face.

It hit the windshield above Alex's head. The bullet's angle didn't completely shatter the glass. Instead, the windshield cracked outward from the bullet hole, becoming a web work of opaque glass crystals.

I couldn't see the road.

I hung on to the wheel with my right hand and slammed my left hand hard into the glass. I was rewarded by bleeding knuckles and a fist-sized view of the terrain beyond the road. I saw the bait shop parking lot. To the right was the shop itself. The corroded propane tank was to the left.

With my left hand back on the steering wheel, I jammed my left foot down on the clutch, shifted into third, and tapped the brakes.

The sniper shot out a tire. Left front.

I used my whole body for leverage, felt pain rip through my right arm as I hauled the wheel to the right.

Still, I couldn't keep the Blazer on the road.

Behind us, death.

Ahead of us, disaster.

Another bullet struck the truck.

Side panel, left rear.

The truck left the road completely, tearing through vines, rocking and jolting as it slewed through the red mud of the parking lot.

Alex cried out. Once.

I kept my eyes focused forward, desperately yanking the steering wheel, trying to avoid the propane tank. Maybe empty. Maybe not.

I continued steering, fighting to maintain some control. I shifted into second and braked again, tried to slow—

Behind us now, enough vine to provide some cover.

I couldn't avoid the old wrecked car in front of us.

It eliminated any further need for braking.

We smashed into it at ten, perhaps fifteen miles per hour.

I collided with the steering wheel.

Hurt.

I didn't have time to worry about it.

The hood buckled. The radiator burst.

But we were stopped.

I looked at Alex.

He was in a crumpled heap on the floor. His eyes were closed. Blood covered his forehead.

My breath caught in my throat.

For a mere heartbeat, I was back in time.

He looked at me through ragged holes cut in the mask.

His eyes were like a cat's—light brown flecked with yellow.

Then he grabbed my arm and wrenched me to my feet.

He pulled me to the car's right rear door.

Blood had spattered the glass, ran down it in rivulets—

No! I had lost enough.

I would *not* lose Alex.

I couldn't help him from where I was.

I pushed open my door, crouched low as I circled around the back of the truck to Alex's door. The smell of petrol told me that the last bullet had punctured the tank.

I pulled Alex across the rubber matting until his hips were

almost at the door, then grabbed him beneath the arms and dragged him from the truck.

His elbow brushed the seat and he groaned.

I half-dragged, half-carried him into the thick vines and weeds behind Willie's Bait Shop.

26

As I pulled him through sharp-edged grass, woody vines, and thorny branches, I assessed Alex's injuries.

There was a knot on his forehead and a bleeding gash. His elbow was a tight, hot, swollen purple shot through with red. The bites on his left arm still bled and now were joined by a growing number of scratches and gouges on both of his arms. His breathing was high-pitched and wheezy.

I dragged Alex five meters. No more.

I hadn't the strength. Or the time.

I abandoned him behind the bait shop, beneath a dying oak, under a tangled, ropy tent of kudzu. His eyes were still closed, but his groaning was louder. I left him, praying that he'd be safe from whatever reptiles might lurk there, knowing that the man who was after us—after me—was infinitely more deadly.

I'd set my trap.

Used myself as bait.

And Alex had become my victim.

The sniper I could take care of myself.

But I needed John. Or someone. Anyone. To help me save Alex.

I ran back to the Blazer, pausing just before I reached it. I stood in the cover provided by the corner of the bait shop, held Alex's semiautomatic, and made sure the shooter hadn't yet arrived.

Still clear.

I moved again, stayed low, and hurried to the truck. I grabbed my purse, dumped it, and retrieved my cigarette lighter.

Minutes, I thought. I had minutes to signal for help.

The air reeked of petrol.

It dripped from the tank, gathered beneath the truck, traveled outward in rivulets. I followed several wet trails with my eyes and chose the puddle nearest me.

I flicked the lighter, produced a flame, touched it to the edge of the puddle, held it there. With a sudden roar, the petrol ignited, flaring violently, scorching my hand and heating my face. I dropped the lighter, flung myself away from the blazing puddle as an orange-blue flame traveled toward the truck.

I ran.

I didn't stop until I reached the corner of the shop. Then I dropped to the ground and peered out at the truck.

In the distance, birds sang.

Overhead, the sky was blue and bright.

The breeze carried the smell of petrol.

I waited.

I watched.

The Blazer exploded.

Flames shot through it, consuming the interior.

Thick, black smoke boiled into the sky.

Pieces of truck rained all around me.

In the midst of it all, I remembered.

Everything.

Sunlight dappled the dusty earth beneath the olive tree. It touched the dark stains on my white dress, dried the wet splashes on my skin.

"Watch her while I get the papers. And then—"

The man who had saved my life turned away, stuck his head and shoulders in through the open door of our car. He reached into the backseat, lifted out my mother's attaché case.

"Messy, but intact. Well done."

He put the case inside the Mercedes, pulled a handkerchief from his pocket, carefully wiped the blood from his hands as he walked back toward us. As he passed our car, he tossed the handkerchief through the open front door, into the front seat.

"Now for our little problem."

For a moment, he stood looking at me through ragged holes cut in the mask. His eyes were almost yellow.

He reached down, grabbed my arm, wrenched me to my feet, pulled me to our car's right rear door, shoved my face against the window.

Blood spattered the glass, ran down it in rivulets. So at first I couldn't see—

Two crumpled bodies. Covered in blood. Gaping flesh where faces had once been.

I didn't *want* to see.

I screamed, threw myself backward, fighting his grasp, fighting to break free.

He held on, lifted me from the ground.

I kicked him, pummeled him with my fists.

I bit him.

He dropped me.

I landed on my feet, ran—

He caught the back of my dress, spun me around, slammed me against the car. He pulled open the back door, forced me into the car, shoved me against the still warm bodies.

I screamed, clawed my way out.

I ran away.

"Talk about this and you'll end up like them," he shouted after me.

I escaped into the olive grove, ran until I stumbled and fell, scrambled forward on all fours, hid behind the nearest tree. I huddled there, fist against my mouth, listening, not making a sound.

Birds sang in the distance. A gentle wind rustled the leaves overhead. Sunlight danced on the dry earth.

Maybe the bad men had gone away.

On hands and knees, I crept from my shelter.

Both cars were still there.

The white one was off the road, among the trees. Broken branches covered its hood, lay across its windshield. The front passenger-side door was open.

The gunman stood beside it, still wearing his mask. Then he held a lighter to a long piece of cloth that hung from the gas tank, waited until it was on fire.

He hurried to the roadside where the black Mercedes was waiting, its motor running, smoky exhaust pouring from its tailpipe. The gunman slid in next to the driver. The car pulled onto the road, roared away, left a cloud of dust and exhaust in its wake.

The smell of petrol carried on the wind.

The white car exploded.

Flames shot through the passenger compartment. Thick, black smoke boiled up into the sky. Pieces of metal rained around me. Stavros's foot hit the ground beside me. It was still encased in a polished black boot. The laces were neatly tied.

I got to my feet. I ran away. Away from the thing on the ground. Away from the smoke and the flames. Away from the men with their masks and their gun. Away from what was inside the white car.

I ran and I ran and I ran.

A stranger was stalking me.

A stranger who was undoubtedly Sir William's henchman. Blond. Burly. Dressed in muddy, olive-colored overalls and a lightweight camouflage jacket. He carried a Kalashnikov submachine gun with an optical sight. Illegal in the States. Which hadn't stopped him from possessing or using it.

I lay flattened beside the low, dilapidated porch, waiting for a clear shot. Alex's SIG-Sauer was in my left hand. My right arm was weak and spasming, almost useless.

The fellow hunkered down low, eyes moving constantly, searching the area between us. The thick smoke and the burning truck made visibility a problem for him and for me.

He came closer, and the breeze cooperated.

There was a moment of clearing.

I began squeezing the trigger.

The deep rumbling roar of an approaching motorcycle sent my quarry diving into the cover of the kudzu vines and interrupted my shot.

The sound grew louder, became stationary, changed to the

sound of a motor idling. Then it cut out with the motorcycle still out of sight somewhere down the road.

John on his Harley, I thought. A good Samaritan would have blundered directly onto the scene. But John would approach cautiously, carrying his bulky Browning, ready to fire. He would creep through the billowing smoke, perhaps end up in the shooter's sights. Perhaps die. More likely, he would kill the fellow with a bullet that didn't come from the SIG-Sauer.

That problem was best avoided.

I crept forward, nearer the burning skeleton of the Blazer. I crawled on forearms and knees, with my chest and stomach dragging, until the heat from the Blazer scorched my skin. I kept my breathing shallow and tried not to inhale too much smoke.

A cough could end my life.

I squinted, tried to penetrate the swirling smoke.

The breeze cooperated again.

Suddenly, I could see the shooter.

He was crouched in a tangle of vine, his attention split between John and me, his submachine gun poised at a point between us, waiting for a target.

I gave him one. But first, I aimed at his head. Any non-lethal shot was too risky, and I didn't know if he was wearing a bulletproof vest.

Then I shouted.

He whipped around as I fired.

His finger was already depressing the trigger, spraying the area with bullets. But he was too late.

His head exploded as the bullet tore through it, front to back.

It was easier to claim self-defense that way.

*   *   *

"All clear," I called.

John came running through the smoke. He paused long enough to kick the Kalashnikov out of the reach of a dead man. Good training.

I turned my back on him, intending to go to Alex.

I made a mistake.

I took a breath at exactly the wrong moment, at the moment that the breeze swirled the smoke around me. I ended up with a lungful.

I doubled over, gasping for air, gagging violently. Pain stabbed through my chest, but I managed to stagger forward another few steps before falling to my knees. I bent forward and wrapped my arms around my chest, trying to protect my rib cage. I cradled my right arm in my left and, despite the agony in my chest, consciously kept the gun in my left hand pointed at the ground.

John's arms kept me from collapsing completely. Suddenly, they were around me, supporting me. He hung on as I worked my way through the pain.

Finally, with eyes still streaming, I turned my head and looked at him.

"You left it a bit late." Cough. "Need help." Cough. "Alex—"

I was seized by another bout of coughing, this one less violent than the last. But I couldn't tell John what I needed until I could drag more oxygen into my lungs.

John held me tight, patted my back, and talked as he waited for the spasm to pass.

"I went for petrol and supplies. I watched the road every minute, except when I went inside to pay. He must have gotten past me then. Sorry, love. You weren't supposed to be here. I thought I left you sleeping—"

He stopped speaking.

Because I was staring at him, half expecting to be staring into the muzzle of a gun.

Of course, there was no gun.

Sorry, love. You weren't supposed to be here.

The voice was so familiar.

This time, he would kill me. Just as he'd killed my mama, my papa, Stavros.

Nonsense. That was the past. A different time. A different man.

The voice.

So familiar.

John's voice.

The same man.

Abruptly, past and present merged with startling clarity.

John was holding me, helping me.

No gun.

No mask.

But I knew.

Alex's semiautomatic was still in my hand.

I pulled away from the support of his arms, lifted the SIG-Sauer. Pointed it point-blank at his face.

"I remember," I said.

He didn't move. Didn't flinch away. He faced death calmly.

I looked at the familiar, narrow features, watched the breeze ruffle his fine blond hair, and knew that I could kill him.

His pale blue eyes remained fixed on my face.

"Your parents were a job. A hit. For the sake of national security."

I stared at him. Stared at the monster my partner—my friend—had kept hidden for all the years I'd known him.

He'd saved my life.

And I'd saved his.

Thus proving our competence. Little else.

Killing him would be easy. I could claim self-defense.

But Alex needed help.

Sooner or later someone would see the smoke and come to investigate. Sooner. Or later. John was here. Now. And I knew he had a cell phone.

I ran my eyes over his slim body, over his dark jeans and olive-drab turtleneck and lightweight jacket. The only telltale bulge was that of his shoulder holster. I saw nothing that was the size and shape of his phone. Perhaps he'd left it in the shack. Or in the Harley's saddlebags. It would take me time to search for it.

In the meantime, Alex suffered.

I lowered the gun.

"Please. Phone for an ambulance. For Alex."

27

He traded me the SIG-Sauer for a phone call.

He held out his hand and said: "Give me the gun, Janie."

I made the deal willingly.

He walked back to the Harley.

I followed the trail of broken vegetation past the back of the bait shop and knelt down beside Alex.

He was feverish, muttering incoherently, fighting for consciousness and not winning. His arm was a nasty mess, purple and swollen from wrist to shoulder. The sleeve of his shirt was stretched tight, the rolled-up cuff digging deeply into his swollen biceps, his veins bulging.

My touch on his arm made him cry out.

Perhaps unconsciousness was a blessing.

I pillowed his head on my lap, stroked back the dark hair that was plastered against his forehead, and waited for John.

"You'll be all right," I murmured over and over again. "You'll be all right."

I wasn't sure I believed my words.

John returned and hunkered down well out of reach. His Browning was in his hand, and he kept it pointed at me. Undoubtedly, he knew that if he let me live, he'd never be safe.

"The ambulance is on the way," he said. "The dispatcher said twenty minutes."

I moved my chin in Alex's direction, intending to use John's sympathy to my advantage and actually fearful that lack of circulation would cause more damage to Alex's arm than the venom had.

"Do you have your pocket knife? I need to cut his shirt away."

John glanced at Alex, then shook his head.

"You're too dangerous to trust, Janie. I'd be foolish to give you a weapon. Especially a knife."

I was good with a throwing knife, and he knew it. I'd once saves his life that way. But under the circumstances—

"For God's sake, you have the fucking gun. Do you think I'd risk—"

His unyielding expression made his thoughts clear.

"You do it, then," I said.

His eyes traveled from my face to Alex's arm and back. Then he pushed a hand covered in supple leather into his back pocket and retrieved his knife. He tossed it to me.

I caught it left-handed, flicked it open, automatically estimated its weight and measured the length of the tapering blade against the length of the hilt. The knife was well balanced enough to be thrown accurately and, if aimed at the right spot, heavy enough to inflict serious damage. I would wait for the right moment and then—

"Jane—"

John waited until I raised my head and met his eyes before moving the point of the Browning. He aimed it at Alex.

"—if you make one wrong move, I'll kill lover boy. You have my word on it."

I nodded and began slicing through the looser fabric at Alex's shoulder. Then I slid the razor-sharp blade, sharp edge upward, down his arm. The taut fabric split easily until the blade reached the folded cuff. I tucked the blade beneath the thick wad of fabric and tugged upward, sawing at the sleeve.

Alex moaned, cried out as the blade nicked him.

I froze for a moment, then kept working.

Finally, I cut through the shirt.

I exhaled and felt my shoulders sag.

John said: "The knife, Janie. Now."

I folded it, threw it back to him, and he returned it to his pocket.

For a time, I sat quietly looking at Alex, grateful that the knotted veins on his forearm were beginning to relax. I watched his chest rise and fall, listened to his wheezing breath, and wondered—

Talking to John was an alternative to worrying about Alex. It was an alternative to worrying about death.

"You work for Sir William."

"Sometimes. And, sometimes, so does Mac. He and William worked together in Greece, decades ago. Even then I think Mac sensed William's corruption. So he sent a young operative digging into Sir William's activities. She was one of Mac's favorites, a woman everyone assumed was nothing more than a career diplomat's pretty little wife. She was a professional. Like you, Janie, but not nearly as tough. She didn't need to be. Or so Mac thought. Which is why, I suspect, he's always been harsher with you. In any event, your mother found something. We'll never know what. Because before she reached Mac, she was murdered."

He met my eyes.

I looked away from him and focused on Alex. His eyelids were beginning to flutter.

"*You* murdered her."

"Sir William said she was a Communist agent who was stealing top secret files and that your father was a weak man, a dupe in her hands."

I defended the parents I didn't know.

"He lied."

"Yes. But I didn't know that then. I simply did my duty."

He paused for a moment, and his matter-of-fact voice was colored with emotion when he added: "Your parents died quickly, Janie. As did the chauffeur. A shot to the head. Just as we were trained. But what Sir William did to you . . . That was brutality."

Tears.

I turned my head, knowing the action betrayed the feelings I wanted to hide.

John kept talking.

"Delphi was my first foreign-duty post. I was barely twenty-three years old, a junior officer assigned to the cultural attaché. I provided intelligence to William and Mac. It was an interesting time—dangerous and volatile. And both men knew how to use history to their advantage. They were intelligent and ruthless and from good families. The sort who rise quickly to positions of power in government service and take loyal subordinates with them. I had ambitions then. But even the silliest bugger grows up. It didn't take me long to realize that Sir William was not driven by the same—"

He paused, held his breath as he searched around for the right words, exhaled when he found them.

"—obsessive sense of duty that is Mac's particular curse. And yours."

I moved to relieve the cramping in my legs, twisted my torso slightly, and gasped as my rib cage objected.

"Please, Jane. Be still. I think you've probably broken a couple ribs."

Concern on his face. Caring. I didn't want it from him.

"Knowing what he is," I said, "you still work for Sir William."

I made it an accusation.

John nodded.

"And you still work for Mac."

No answer for that.

John didn't seem to expect one.

"After you and I returned from Scotland, Sir William ordered me to kill you. I was shocked, really, to discover I couldn't. It was simply . . . wrong. And you've come to mean far too much—"

He shook his head, interrupted the thought.

"I told Sir William to bugger himself. So he dispatched someone more reliable. Someone not so old and soft, he told me. You survived the fire, disappeared. I was relieved. And I was off the hook. I told myself that you'd manage on your own, as you always have. I thought you'd never recognize me, even if you *did* remember everything else. So it was none of my business, really. Then Mac called. In the end, I followed you here."

"You came here to *protect* me?"

"I fired that shot from on top of the market to encourage you to protect yourself. And I wanted the police involved. Callaghan loves you. Probably always has. I didn't understand why a dozen cops weren't out there, protecting you. I still don't."

He paused, but I offered no explanation.

Alex moved his head, muttered my name.

John glanced at him, then refocused on me.

"I showed up on your doorstep offering my services and intending to eliminate the immediate threat. Nothing more. Unfortunately, circumstances have changed."

Sirens wailed in the distance.

Help for Alex. Thank God.

John stood, stepped toward us, looked down at me as he had so many years earlier. This time he wore no mask. But he still held a gun. It pointed unwaveringly at my face.

This time, I wasn't a terrified child.

I ignored the dark view down the barrel and kept my eyes on John's.

"Go on," I said. "Finish what you started. Just leave Alex unharmed. Please. You owe me that much."

Then he nodded, and I tensed, waiting—

Then he did something inexplicable. He holstered the Browning, slipped the SIG-Sauer from his jacket pocket, and handed it to me.

"Circumstances change. I find that I'm inclined to go back to London and visit my employer."

He stood quietly, facing me. Then he turned and walked slowly away.

I held the gun, aimed it at his back.

I couldn't pull the trigger.

I should hate him, I thought.

I didn't.

I understood too well the twisted morality of our profession.

John paused when he reached the corner of the bait shop.

"Goodbye, love," he said clearly.

A minute later, I heard the roar of the Harley's engine as he rode away.

The ambulance arrived.

The paramedics spotted the body and called the cops.

The cops arrived as Alex and I were loaded into the back of the ambulance. Redheaded Merle, bulky Buchannan, and two rookies I didn't know. They called Tommy and remained at the scene.

The ambulance wailed its way to the hospital.

I reached over, took Alex's hand, and was surprised to receive a squeeze in return.

Tommy met us at the emergency room door, leaned over Alex's stretcher.

"Damn it, man. Snake bit? Can't you *ever* stay out of trouble?"

Alex found enough strength to shift the mask away from his mouth and found enough oxygen to wheeze out an answer.

"Guess not."

The paramedics took him through a familiar set of swinging doors.

This time, I knew he would live.

When Tommy leaned over my stretcher, he had his cop-face on.

I didn't wait for him to ask questions. I volunteered information.

"I killed that fellow after he'd ambushed Alex and me. Payback, I think, from one of my old enemies."

Tommy's hostile expression melted into a friend's concern.

"There'll be an investigation."

I nodded, smiled up at him.

"No problem. I plan on staying."

28

A week later, the ringing phone awakened us at dawn.

Damned phone.

Alex grabbed it, favoring his bandaged arm.

"For you," he said.

He waited for me to work myself into an upright position. The strapping on my ribs slowed me down.

"William is dead," Mac said without preamble.

"How?"

I tried to keep my voice neutral, but something in that single word must have betrayed some emotion.

Alex's eyes darted back to me. His expression was alert, worried.

Though I thought he'd probably guessed, I'd already told Alex the situation with Sir William was resolved. I'd trusted him not to ask questions.

Now, I flashed Alex a smile as I listened to Mac.

"Apparently the nephew killed him. It happened a few hours ago. Hugh had been home from the sanatorium for less than a week and practically took his uncle's head off with a bird gun. Of course, he maintains that he was sleeping when it happened. He told the police he found his uncle dead in the study and that obviously it was an accident. There *were* cleaning supplies spread across William's desk. But the angle of entry was completely wrong and the cleaning supplies were laid out *on top of* the blood spattering. Stupid, greedy little sod. He'll probably spend the rest of his life in some mental hospital."

Mac paused for a moment, then said: "You can come home, Janie."

"No need. I already am."

There was little to say after that. Except goodbye.

I hung up the phone, thinking that John had an exquisite sense of justice.

"What's wrong?" Alex said.

Pure anxiety.

I cuddled in beside him.

"Nothing. Except, now that we're both awake, I was wondering . . ."

I raised an eyebrow and loaded my voice with pure lust.

"Oh, yeah," he said.

He rolled onto his side, faced me, carefully shifted his bandaged left arm, and laid it along the top of my pillow. He tried not to flinch as he moved it.

I pouted.

"I don't suppose we'll ever make love when one of us *isn't* injured?"

He lowered his head and brushed my lips with his.

"Be grateful," he murmured. "This particular injury means we can spend some quality time together."

"Define quality."

He slid his right hand beneath the sheet, trailed his fingers down my belly, and demonstrated.

I moaned softly.

Then he moved his hand and slipped it behind my neck. Color touched the ridge of his cheeks. Above them, his dark eyes were dilated. He pulled my face close to his, trailed the tip of his tongue along the cup of my ear, and half-breathed, half-whispered to me.

"If you'll allow me to demonstrate, I think you will find—"

He nipped at my cheek.

"—my right-handed technique—"

He ran the tip of his tongue along my lower lip.

"—quite satisfactory."

A while later, I repeated Alex's words, imitating his drawl, creating a lingering verbal caress.

"Quite satisfactory. Ah'm sure."

SPRING

29

Alex and I sat in the living room, in front of the telly, dressed much alike—old jeans and faded SPD T-shirts. The French doors were open wide to catch the afternoon breeze. Outside, the sun was shining, the birds singing, and the magnolias were in full bloom.

We had our feet up on the coffee table and our hands around frosty mint juleps. In fifteen minutes, the Kentucky Derby would run.

The phone rang in the kitchen. Alex left me to answer it.

He came back ten minutes later, sat down beside me, and took a sip of his drink.

"That was the local sheriff in a little river town down near the Shawnee National Forest," he said. "Southern Illinois. That's where the Feds relocated Willie. I called a friend in the DEA a while ago, just like you suggested. I told him I needed to know how Willie was getting along. He called the sheriff. The sheriff called me. He says he knew Willie—by his new name, of course. Willie got himself a nice house with a river full of fish practically off the back steps."

I smiled.

"A happy ending."

"Yeah. Except for one thing. According to the sheriff, they all had some real bad flooding last year. The levy looked like it might give way. Willie was there, along with most of the town, helping them sandbag. Seems he fell into the river and drowned."

I stared at Alex, opened my mouth to ask—

He shook his head.

"Best to let it be," he said.

Then he snuggled in close, and the Derby began.